Don G. Porter

McRoy & Blackburn
Publishers

Elmer E. Rasmuson Library Cataloging in Publication Data:
Porter, Don G.
Happy hour / Don G. Porter. Ester, Alaska : McRoy & Blackburn, c2005.

p. cm.
ISBN 0-9706712-53
1. Alaska—Fairbanks—Fiction. 2. Alaska—Anchorage—Fiction. 3. Alaska—Bethel—Fiction. 4. Alaska—Grayling—Fiction. I. Title.

PS3616.O777 H37 2005
Printed in Canada

McRoy and Blackburn, Publishers
PO Box 276
Ester, Alaska 99725
www.alaskafiction.com

Book and cover design and layout by Sue and Russ Mitchell, Inkworks.

Hey, Honey, How do You Spell "Acknowledgements"?

Writing is said to be a lonely occupation, but I haven't found it so. My lovely young wife Deborah is an artist who works with her back to me across a large room, but close enough for shouting; "Honey, what was the name of that . . .?" or "How do you spell . . .?" And at whatever distance, she gracefully accepts: "I'll be along at the end of this chapter."

Behind every book is an editor who pushes the author just to the edge of distraction, but never over. In this case it's Carla Helfferich who minded the p's and q's and insisted on accuracy in every sentence. She's also the one who transforms a shapeless pile of coffee-stained papers into a book.

You would not be reading this without the tireless efforts of my agent, Pia Hoffman, at the Sunshine Agency. She keeps mailing out manuscripts and chirps, "Don't get discouraged; I'm not."

I'm actually an imposter when I claim to have written a book, because my efforts are team products: my support group is in constant e-mail contact, reading, revising, suggesting, editing. I hope you know some of them. There's Ivan Pierce, author of *An Infantry Lieutenant's Vietnam* and the upcoming *Missing In Cordova,* and also William (Bill) Marsik, author of the soon-to-be-released *Gemini,* but also a gold mining partner from the Alaska days and the model for several of my characters.

Remember in grade school, those girls who got everything right and made the boys look dumb? I have two of those, still at it: Joann Condit and C. J. Seidlitz, both professional editors, and I don't sign my name without passing it by one or both of them.

Three of my sons offer support and advice. That's Don F., Ron, and Greg, all of whom will soon leave the old man in their literary dust. My favorite sister-in-law, Pat Porter, whipped out my web site in twenty minutes.

You know what they say about the tip of the iceberg, and that was it. Thirty members of my extended family are in constant e-mail contact. Several are the type who read one or more books every week. They circumnavigate the globe on a daily basis and compete with each other to answer questions. Want to know the color of the first Arctic Cat? The temperature of the hot springs where folks swim in Antarctica? Fastest way to get from Heathrow to Hyde Park? How to get a wheelchair on top the Great Wall of China? Speed limit on the Kansas Turnpike? Type of trees around the campus at the University of Alaska, or in Caracas? Ask at night and have six answers in the morning. Furthermore, they're waiting for this book and may even buy a copy.

Obviously there isn't room to name them all, but a typical example of constant support and encouragement is Bev Larsen, president, first, and so far only, member of my fan club.

Thanks, guys.

Chapter 1

In another five minutes I'd have been out of radio range, but Vickie nailed me. "Eight-Four Zulu, Renaldo's on the phone. He has a public relations problem and needs your help ASAP."

I said what I always say when Renaldo has an emergency. "Roger, tell him I'll be over on the evening jet."

By "public relations problem," Renaldo meant that someone was threatening to kill him. That statement was a code for us; it translated that if I wanted to see him alive again, I'd better do it now. He seemed to attract that kind of problem because he had an obsession with becoming a millionaire. That kept him playing in the big leagues, and a lot of players there were not nice people. There are nice millionaires, several of them actually in Bethel, and very good people well on their way by honorable means, but Renaldo never seemed to meet those types.

Renaldo himself was nice people, maybe too nice. Notice, I'm not saying he's naive, just optimistic, and I guess that's what kept me playing Mr. Hyde to his Dr. Jekyll. We'd always been opposites, right from the first day we found ourselves roommates in college. Renaldo was a fancy dresser, wearing his hair in forty-dollar razor cuts and getting manicures, and he was a serious student of economics because he already had his obsession with becoming a millionaire.

I was sliding through college on a football scholarship, filling in the off-season on the boxing team. I got five-dollar taper-and-fade haircuts only on special occasions.

I drifted into accounting because Renaldo helped me and made it seem easy, but I already had my student pilot's license, and my dream ended with becoming an airline captain. Those college years were formative, and maybe because we were opposites, we formed a kind of symbiosis: Renaldo's brain, my muscles. College friendships run deep, and since neither of us had a brother, maybe we filled a void for each other. In any case, whenever he called, it never occurred to me not to go.

In college, his problems usually started when some girl dumped her foot-ball-jock boyfriend and latched onto Renaldo. It was never Renaldo's fault; he never went looking for girls or trouble, they seemed to come looking for him. Renaldo fended off the girls; I convinced the jocks that they didn't want to hassle Renaldo.

His problems have escalated considerably since then. I picked up my private detective license because the Alaska State Troopers are steady charter customers and the license facilitates some situations. For instance, it makes it quasi-legitimate for me to handle evidence and, on rare occasions, make arrests. One of the perks is a permit to carry a concealed weapon, and that has a lot to do with Renaldo's still being alive.

When Vickie called, I was en route to Grayling, two hundred miles north of Bethel on the Yukon River. Mary Peterson was sitting beside me, all gussied up for a trip to town in a flowered housedress, her raven-black hair carefully braided and wound into a crown. Mary was Indian, not Eskimo, precisely because she was from Grayling, but she had the softer, rounder Eskimo features that sometimes crop up along the borders between the two nations.

That's less likely than it sounds, because it's only been a few generations since Eskimos and Indians killed each other on sight, but genes do have a way of migrating across most any border. The hatchet is buried now, so to speak, and the borders are blurring. Aniak, on the Kuskokwim River, is on a border, and the village athletic teams proudly call themselves the Half-Breeds. As a pacifist, I like that a lot.

Two of Mary's daughters, twelve-year-old Angie and ten-year-old Mandy, were buried in groceries in the seats behind us. The girls were dressed for the special trip to town in matching pinafores, white socks, and patent leather shoes with buckles. They both wore pigtails with ribbons and rapt expressions that indicated they were on an adventure. Tan apple cheeks blushed crimson highlights from the excitement of having gone to town. "Town" is a relative term. Very few people would call Bethel, with 5,000 inhabitants, a town, but to Angie and Mandy it was awesome.

I'd taken the two rear seats out of the Cessna 206 and packed sacks of groceries two layers deep from the bulkhead to the back of the middle seats. Then we got the girls buckled in, carefully arranging their skirts to avoid wrinkles, and packed grocery sacks around and between them. Mary, in the co-pilot's seat, had the final sack of ten dozen eggs in her lap.

Mary made a grocery run to Bethel every three months, and made it count because the charter fare was three hundred bucks. Bushmaster's promise to our customers was that if they could get it to the airport in one taxi, we could get it to the village in a Cessna 206. Village ladies were very good at judging just how many sacks of groceries could possibly be squeezed into the cabin.

It was the kind of afternoon that Robert Service was rhapsodizing about when he penned, "The summers no sweeter were ever . . ." From 3,000 feet, we could see the rugged, snow-covered Russian Mountains fifty miles to our right, and the Alaska Range beyond them. These particular Russian Mountains are not in Russia; they're on the Kuskokwim River between Crooked Creek and Aniak. Gentle hills grew up ahead of us, looking fuzzy because of new yellow-green leaves that were sprouting everywhere.

The flat tundra of the Delta gave way to hills with serious mountains behind them; the Yukon stopped its meandering, constricted to the path it had gored through the mountains. We dropped down to fly right up the river for the last twenty miles. The Yukon, lined with tall spruce and dotted with gravel bars, was working its way out of the Kaiyuh Mountains.

The gravel bars were sprouting one- and two-year-old willows, and the young trees were favorite moose feed. We'd just spotted a pair of cows with three calves, enjoying the afternoon sunshine and munching new leaves.

Angie piped up from the back seat. "Look, mama, just like our family, a mama, a daddy, and three kids." The third sibling she referred to was an older brother, now living in Bethel, and they had probably just visited him. I didn't think it was my place to point out that both adult moose were cows. The bull was up in the mountains by himself without the least interest in calves, and only a seasonal one in cows. She'll find out about male proclivities soon enough.

She was distracted by a big black bear that was industriously slapping a salmon out of the water on the end of an island. The salmon was two feet long, shimmering silver, and putting up a heck of a fight. "Look, that bear's got dinner. Come on, bear, nail him down."

Mandy saw it differently. "Not fair, the bear is too big. Come on, salmon, come on salmon, one more jump."

"Get him, get him, he's getting away." The struggle was in six inches of water on the edge of the gravel and it looked like a geyser erupting.

"Come on salmon, go, go, go."

The bear batted the salmon four feet up onto the bank, got both paws on top of him and nearly bit him in two before the big fish could make it back to the water. Mandy was crushed. "It's just not fair, the bigger ones always win." I wondered if she were speaking for all younger siblings.

A conical hill, bristling with spruce trees, came right to the riverbank, and behind it the Grayling runway perched on a gravel shelf. It's a good dirt strip, twelve hundred feet long, but it has a hill at each end, so you approach it sideways over the river. The windsock is on the village end, a bright orange cone that was swinging lazily back and forth, indicating a ten-knot wind from the north.

We stayed ten feet off the river and, to announce our arrival, flew past the log cabins scattered along the riverbank. The villagers would recognize the airplane and know who was supposed to meet us. I backed off power and pulled us up a hundred feet to lose some speed, swung over the trees on our left toward the mountain, then pulled us around in a tight turn, over the river and back past the village. Mary's husband had come out of their log cabin and was climbing into his pickup when we passed the village again.

"Darn that man. He was supposed to take in the laundry but it's still on the line. I'll probably have to wash it all over." Little touch of pride in her voice. Her husband was untamed and untamable.

I dropped twenty degrees of flaps and trimmed for seventy-five knots. The river at the lower end of the strip was half a mile wide, enough for a two-minute turn, safe and comfortable at seventy-five. A hundred-foot approach had been cleared through the trees between the hill and the strip to let us line up. I chopped the power, slid the pitch control to high RPM, and cranked the trim tab right on up to sixty knots. Thirty feet from the end of the strip, I dropped another ten degrees of flaps and we were rolling on the smooth dirt runway. My watch said 4:30; I'd be back in Bethel by 6:00, with two hours to catch the evening jet and find out who was trying to kill Renaldo this time, and why.

Mary's husband came bumping down the trail through the spruce trees from the village in his battered old blue Ford pickup. We loaded the sacks in back, packing them around the girls again. Mandy seemed to have an affinity for a particular sack, and I noticed one of those net bags that grapes come in was suspiciously open at the top. Mary climbed in the front seat of the pickup, still clutching her eggs, and I was closing the back doors on the airplane, when Agnes, the village health aide, came roaring out of the woods riding a three-wheeler. The way her black hair and summer parka streamed out in the wind behind her conjured the image of a witch on a broom, but that was only her physical aspect. Agnes was a sweetheart, had been the village health aide for twenty years. To my personal knowledge, she had saved at least a dozen lives.

Agnes slid her green three-wheeler to a stop under the wing with a shower of gravel. Normally she would have been smiling, but her pleasant, round, weather-tanned face was set in hard serious lines that indicated she was on an important mission at the moment.

"Hey, Alex, Vickie just called on the single sideband. There's a medical emergency at Holy Cross and you're the closest airplane."

"Thanks, Aggie, I'm on the way. I'll come up to the house for a piece of your cranberry pie next trip. What's the emergency?"

"Vickie didn't say. We were afraid I couldn't catch you in time. Nana is expecting you."

"Nana" is a nickname for the health aide at Holy Cross. It means 'aunt' and it's about as affectionate as a name can get.

"Aggie, you can catch me any old time." I couldn't resist laying a little blarney on her. Aggie was around sixty years old, and somehow that made it okay to flirt outrageously with her. I blew her a kiss; she ignored my overtures but was losing the battle to suppress a grin. She backed her machine around and bounded away toward the village with a roar from her unmuffled five-horse engine.

With no load and half-tanks of fuel, there was no need to taxi back for a take off into the wind. I turned around, dropped twenty degrees of flap and shot the juice to her. That three-hundred-horse IO 540 snapped right to red line. The plane was flying in six hundred feet, and I headed back down the river. "Medical emergency" is number one priority in the charter business. A lot of village emergencies involve chainsaws, boat propellers, occasionally a gunshot wound. The village health aides are good at first aid, but the nearest blood transfusions are in Bethel, and getting a patient there fast could mean life or death. Holy Cross was on the Yukon, almost on my way home, so I could still make the evening jet.

The reason Aggie made her dash was that I'd have passed Holy Cross before I was in radio range of Bethel. The airplane radio is VHF, and that's limited to line of sight, so I'd have had to turn around and lose precious time, but every village clinic has a single sideband radio in the HF band. They can all talk to each other and to the Bethel hospital. Every charter service has a similar radio. Normally, each service uses its own frequencies so they don't hear each other, but they can switch frequencies and talk to anyone.

I climbed up to five hundred feet, just high enough to make a straight line over the hills when the river turned. Holy Cross nestles behind a rise where the river swings away from the hills. I flew straight across the village to alert

Nana that I was there, chopped the power and lowered flaps on the downwind leg over the river. With no passengers, it was okay to horse the plane around to land back toward the village, into the wind. The runway is downriver from the village on a flat shelf between the river and the mountain.

Nana was waiting by the equipment shed when I pulled off the dirt runway at the intersection of the airport and the lane into the village. Two women, one large, one small, were leaning against an old abandoned road grader that made a rusting yellow gash through the green willows. The women looked like exotic tropical flowers in red corduroy *kuspuks*.

The kuspuk is an A-line outer garment that's used as a summer parka, and the women were sitting with their hoods up and their hands tucked into their sleeves to make the smallest possible targets for mosquitoes. When I opened the door, I could smell the village that lay upwind, a quarter-mile away through the trees. It's a clean, not unpleasant smell of wood smoke, animal hides, and drying fish. Nana led a little girl, ten or twelve years old, by the hand, and the girl was walking strangely. I thought maybe she'd sprained an ankle or twisted a knee.

"Hi, Alex, this is Anna. You need to get her to the hospital as fast as possible."

"Sure thing. Hi, Anna. Do you want to sit in front or in back?" Anna had the biggest eyes I'd ever seen on a little girl, the pupils so black that the irises didn't show. Her little round face was an impassive mask, as though her spirit had left her body to escape the pain. I'm not an expert on Eskimo techniques, but that analogy may be close to true. Her body was suffering, but her psyche had retreated to a safe place.

"Better put her in back. She'll need both seats; she can't sit up straight. Her Auntie Ethel will meet you at the hospital."

Anna wasn't making a sound. Eskimo stoicism starts early. No whimpering, and they don't talk unless they have something to say. Sometimes I think our culture could benefit from that. She got her left foot up on the step, but her right leg seemed to be too stiff to make the next step. I picked her up and set her in the back seat. She immediately rolled over to lie across both seats.

"What's her problem?" I could see that Anna was in pain, but hadn't figured out why.

"She cut herself. Bunch of kids were roughhousing and Anna sat down hard on a broken bottle. Get her in fast, Alex. She's losing blood and needs a painkiller. All I have is aspirin."

We left the Yukon and the mountains to angle across bare flat tundra for the one-hour dash to Bethel on the Kuskokwim River. I stayed at one hundred feet and made a beeline, using the low frequency, nondirectional beacon to keep us straight toward Bethel. What wind there was, was right behind us, and I set a high-end cruise at 2600 RPM, so we were making 165 knots, but there's an awful lot of flat tundra and a jillion tiny lakes between the Yukon and the Kuskokwim at Bethel.

I could have called ahead for an ambulance, but when I glanced back at Anna she looked terrified. If she could have sat up and looked out the window, the nesting swans and geese and the occasional beaver dams and moose we passed might have distracted her, but she was lying across the seats, teeth clenched, and staring at the back of my seat. I figured that a bunch of strangers in white coats with flashing lights and sirens would be a trauma she didn't need. It would be just as fast, maybe faster, to put her in the seat of my old International pickup. I called for a straight-in approach. That was downwind, but with a mile and a half of runway in Bethel, it didn't matter. After I taxied in, I locked the brake and left the plane next to the parking lot for someone else to put away. Anna lay down in the pickup seat and rested her head on my thigh.

At that point, I thought that was a good thing because it meant she had decided to trust me. She probably recognized me. There are usually a bunch of kids hanging around the village airports, and they have the recognition advantage. There's only one pilot at a time, so he's easy to pick out. In any case, I was her link to Holy Cross. I knew where she belonged and how to get her back there.

I carried her up the steps into the hospital and stood her up in front of the reception desk. I'd been right not to call an ambulance; Anna was near panic anyway. We were standing in the biggest, brightest room that she had ever seen, and there were strange *gussaks* (which is what she'd call Caucasians) running around. The ambient noise level—phones ringing, radios squawking, fifty people talking in the lobby—probably sounded like a riot to Anna. Her mouth dropped open and her eyes were so wide that her lashes were merged with her brows.

Nana had called ahead, so the paperwork was all done, but I didn't see Auntie Ethel anywhere. The nurse who rushed to meet us was Bobbie. In her early thirties, she was the sweetest, kindest, least threatening personage since Florence Nightingale, but she did have blonde hair, and Anna might never have seen that before. When I tried to hand Anna to Bobbie, the child grabbed onto my ring finger with a grip you'd expect from a professional wrestler. When I looked down, her fist and my finger were turning white. I let the finger lead us, and we followed Bobbie down the hall.

My watch said 6:45, forty-five minutes left until check-in time for the jet, and still no Auntie Ethel. Bobbie led us into an exam room and had to lift Anna onto the table by herself. I couldn't help, because I was still one-handed. Bobbie folded Anna's kuspuk up above her waist and used a pair of scissors to snip off her jeans. She removed a blood-soaked white hand towel from Anna's leg and gently peeled a bandage the size of a pancake off her right hip.

Bobbie gasped and ran out of the room. My stomach did a flip. The cut was round, the size of the bottom of a bottle, but the way the skin gaped away, you could see that it was inches deep. Bobbie was back in ten seconds, towing a doctor. The doctor already had the needle in his hand. He swabbed a clean spot and gave Anna a shot. I felt the tension go out of her body, but the grip on my finger didn't loosen.

Bobbie went to work, swabbing and scrubbing. When she reached in with a pair of needle-nosed pliers (no doubt called by another name in medical circles) and pulled out pieces of brown glass, I had to look away. Anna was calmer; her eyes were at half-mast, showing only the black pearls of her pupils, but she wasn't releasing her grip. I heard the jet land at the airport, five miles away, because the pilots use full power against the reverse thrusters to stop.

Bobbie finished her ministrations, taped on a big chunk of gauze, and covered Anna with a white cloth, only there was a neat round hole in the cloth so it didn't cover the gauze. We wheeled the cart out into the hall, Bobbie pulling, me following my finger, and turned toward what I suppose was an operating room. We had made ten feet down the hall when the front doors banged open and pandemonium erupted at the reception desk.

Two city cops, approximately two hundred pounds each, were struggling to hold an obviously very drunk little woman between them. The cops were being whipped back and forth like a couple of toys, and the receptionist set off an alarm bell. White coats materialized from every direction. Bobbie deserted us to join the fray, and six or eight people finally held the woman still enough for a doctor to inject her with something.

The commotion tapered off fast; the cops gave the medics a quick rundown and fled. Bobbie got up from her seat on the woman's back and returned to wheel the cart. I had to ask. Bobbie was shaking her head "no," but she whispered, "Her boyfriend caught her cheating and put Drano in her douche bag."

My wristwatch had shifted into overdrive. Somehow, it had leapt ahead to 7:30. I could feel Renaldo pulling me toward the jet and Anchorage. I had to cut and run, had to get to Renaldo, but I could not bring myself to jerk my finger away from Anna. We were wheeling right along down the polished tile hallway, at least a city block from the entrance, and I was getting frantic.

We had just come to the end of the hallway, ready to turn right toward surgery or left toward the clinic, when the front door burst open and Auntie Ethel came sprinting down the hall. She was dressed in heels and hose, which mean only one thing in Bethel. Nana had neglected to mention that Auntie Ethel was coming in on the evening jet from Anchorage. Anna was very nearly unconscious, but she recognized Auntie Ethel, and allowed me to peel my finger out of the Chinese finger trap. We inserted Auntie Ethel's finger, and I ran for the pickup.

It's five miles through the tundra from the Bethel hospital to the airport. It's a state highway, the only paved road west of Anchorage, so the speed limit is fifty-five. I was hitting eighty when I skidded around the bend past the end of the airport with half a mile to go. It was just 8 PM. Normally, the jet would have left half an hour late, but not that night. It taxied away from the terminal and lumbered out onto the runway. I clamped on the binders and skidded into Bushmaster's parking lot.

Vickie looked up and furrowed her forehead into an uncharacteristic frown. She was wearing a white blouse, dark skirt, heels and hose, all very classy by Bethel standards, but her honey-blonde bob was showing the effects of a long day and many phone calls; I expect her disposition was, too.

"I thought you were going out on the jet." She knew what a call from Renaldo meant to me and my schedule. She wouldn't have been surprised if the office didn't see me again for a week or more.

"Yeah, well, the best laid plans of mice and men. Is the 310 scheduled for anything?"

The jet took off. Everything stopped while thunder shook the office.

Vickie ran a ruby-tipped finger down the schedule book and gave a negative shake of her bob. Vickie was a very attractive woman, and you may get the idea that I had a thing for her. I don't deny that. Everyone had a thing for Vickie, but don't get carried away. She was my partner's wife.

The Cessna 310 had sort of fallen through the cracks. If we needed a fast twin to move half a dozen geologists from St. Lawrence Island to Prudhoe Bay, we used the Beech B-50. We used the single-engine Cessna 206s, 207s, or 185s for village work because they were cheaper. For serious freight hauling, we used the tri-motor or the American Pilgrim, but the 310 was just right for scooting me to Anchorage. I tossed my flight bag into the back seat and followed the jet.

Chapter 2

The 310 did its homesick angel impersonation while I filed a flight plan: direct Anchorage. I leveled off at ten thousand feet, synchronized the engines, and rolled onto the sixty-degree VOR radial, outbound from Bethel. At 8:30 in the evening, the sun was nearing the horizon to the northwest, but not going down; it was scooting along the horizon sideways. I left the Delta behind and crossed the Kilbuck Mountains, which morphed into the Kuskokwim Mountains.

The snow-covered Russian Mountains were on my left now, starting to pick up sunset colors. The Holitna Valley passed, running north and south toward its rendezvous with the Kuskokwim, and the Alaska Range started growing up like a serrated wall in front of me. The Stony River made a crooked silver thread on the left, and I could see a couple of yard lights, ten miles away, at the BIA school in Lime Village.

Snow on the Alaska Range was turning pink and orange and getting darker. I ran on up to twelve thousand feet, which gave me a two-thousand-foot buffer over the mountains ahead. You don't want to stay that high for too long, because there isn't much oxygen up there. On the other hand, you don't want to trim too close over the mountains when it's getting dark. As most pilots know, and some dead pilots didn't know, your altimeter can be wrong by a thousand feet when you're more than a hundred miles from a reporting station. The altimeter is a sensitive barometer, calibrated in feet and perfectly accurate, so long as you know what the barometric pressure is on the ground below you. I had a canister of oxygen under my seat, like a miniature scuba tank, but that's for emergencies when you start to see things that aren't there.

The sun finally made its dive, leaving sunset colors in the north and the mountains turning to silhouettes. I picked up the Anchorage VOR but it was blinking on and off because mountains were blocking it. I was above the mountains, with an extra thousand feet just in case the altimeter was wrong, but Anchorage is at sea level, so mountains were still between us. Looking down at those mountains is like looking down at a gravel pile, but the rocks are ten thousand feet tall with nearly vertical walls disappearing into black canyons thousands of feet deep.

When you bust out of the Alaska Range in the dark and see Anchorage spread out on the other side of the Knik Arm, it looks like a blanket of stars. Anchorage fills the ten-mile strip from Cook Inlet to the Chugach Mountains and runs two thousand feet up the slopes. On the left, the Matanuska Valley leads north between the Alaska Range and the Chugach Range. Anchorage tapers to darkness, with the city of Palmer making a bubble of light forty miles up the valley.

On the right, Anchorage comes to an abrupt halt at Turnagain Arm. Beyond the arm and the Fire Island FAA facility, the Kenai Peninsula is a dark mat floating on lighter water, with the city of Kenai a glow in the sky fifty miles down the coast. A bright orange necklace of burning gas flares from the oil rigs leads down Cook Inlet past Kenai toward Kodiak Island.

I chopped the power when I passed the black silhouette of Mt. Spur, the volcano on the eastern edge of the Alaska Range that covered Anchorage with six inches of ash in the 1950s. I had to lose twelve thousand feet of altitude in forty miles, so it was all downhill from there. Ahead of me, right in the middle of the growing star field, Renaldo was no doubt tending his new bar. He wouldn't have called me unless he had a serious problem. The kinds of problems that Renaldo called me for were apt to get pretty physical, and likely as not would involve the .357 magnum revolver that I carry in my flight bag.

Having Renaldo in Anchorage was a convenient change. His quest for riches had led him from South America to Greenland and from Europe to Guam, and I'd blasted him out of trouble in half of his ventures. When Renaldo met Gustave in Seattle, and bought his Malamute Saloon, one of Anchorage's Fourth Avenue bars, for fifty thousand dollars, I knew there was going to be trouble.

Dense as I am, I have learned that when something is too good to be true, it's not. Bright as Renaldo is, he never seemed to learn that lesson. Gustave's selling a bar for fifty thousand that was worth a half million raised my hackles, but Renaldo just thought that his ship had finally come in. Now, a month later, we were going to find out what his ship was carrying.

Merrill Field is the municipal airport. The tower specified a Ship Creek approach. I drifted down over Ship Creek and the railroad yards, made the turn over a solid carpet of lights and traffic, kissed the lighted, paved runway, and tied the 310 to a cable behind Wilbur's Flight Service. Joe and Anne Wilbur have been running that facility for a good many years, although Anne still looks to be in her twenties. Anyhow, they provide transient tie-downs with the understanding that you buy your gasoline from them when you leave. I was going to need seventy-five gallons, so no problem.

No matter how many times you do it, it takes a while to adjust from the Bush to the stream of traffic that seemed to be racing on the six lanes of Fifth Avenue. Streetlights lit the cataract of traffic at least as bright as daylight. With the airport behind me, the city around me, and the raging river of cars going by, I was in culture shock.

If you go west from Anchorage, back the way I had just come, you won't see lights like Anchorage again until you've gone a thousand miles around the world to Vladivostok. The air seemed to be mostly exhaust, and it stung my eyes for a while before I got used to it. It was like the smell of a village; you notice it coming in, but once you're in it, you don't notice it anymore.

A pushbutton on a lamppost by the crosswalk stopped about a thousand cars while I strolled across the street toward the twenty-four-hour Airport Café to call a taxi. The sign on the cafe announcing "Peggy's Pies" was tempting. I suddenly remembered that I hadn't eaten since I wolfed a sandwich between Tuntatuliak and Bethel nine hours before, but duty called.

The cab was a sleek new Pontiac, bright yellow, but covered with black phone numbers. The driver was apparently psychic. He snapped on headlights and screeched up beside me the instant I survived the street crossing.

"Need a cab?" He had the uniform cap and jacket, gray hair curling from under the cap behind, but he looked like the battered extras you see hanging around gymnasiums in fight movies.

I climbed in back; this was not a guy I wanted to chat with. "Fourth Avenue and E Street."

When he heard the destination, he turned around, gave me a lascivious wink. "Looking for a little action?"

"I sincerely hope not," I told him.

We barged into the traffic and were doing sixty miles an hour with cars close enough to touch on all four sides of us. Fifth Avenue took us straight into the center of town. Car lots graduated into low office buildings, and eventually we were passing tall steel and glass, but the buildings were mostly dark until we wheeled around the corner from E Street and turned back toward the airport on Fourth Avenue. Fourth had one- and two-story buildings but was brightly lit and bustling, at least from my point of view.

On the Delta, and throughout most of Alaska, the average village has less than five hundred inhabitants. Bethel, with a nominal five thousand, is the biggest city in an area the size of Oregon, so Anchorage with a quarter-million people looked pretty big to me. If you're coming the other way, from the Lower 48, you'd probably consider Anchorage a small town.

The other thing about Anchorage that made it stand out was that most of the people on the sidewalks and milling in and out of the bars were obviously, gloriously, drunk. Liquor is a way of life in Alaska, with consumption per person around twice the national average. However, each municipality and village may vote itself wet or dry.

Almost all villages are dry, and with very good reason. It may not be politically correct to notice anymore, but it used to be common knowledge that the Eskimo, like the American Indian, has a low tolerance for alcohol. Firewater hasn't been around long enough for them to build up a tolerance. If your roots are in the other hemisphere, your ancestors have mostly been alcoholics for several thousand years. You still get addicted, but dealing with the poison is built into your genes.

It's not that the Eskimos and Indians didn't try. They knew what to smoke, what to munch, and what to drink to alter consciousness, but they hadn't produced anything in the quantities and the potency of what was flowing on Fourth Avenue.

Bethel, traditionally, has been voted wet for two years, then dry for two. A large portion of the population is transient, with doctors, lawyers, teachers, and government functionaries assigned to Bethel for four years. New arrivals can't believe the problems, and they want their booze, so they vote wet. Two years later, when they've seen the deaths and heartaches that liquor causes in Bethel, they vote it dry again. However, Anchorage was, and always has been, very, very wet.

The taxi meter said twelve bucks, so I handed the driver fifteen and collected another lascivious, knowing wink. He barged into the stream of crowding, weaving traffic on the street and I barged into the stream of crowding, weaving traffic on the sidewalk. Renaldo's bar was the fourth on the right. There aren't any bars on the left, or north, side anymore since the 1964 earthquake dumped that side of Fourth Avenue down the hill onto Third Avenue, but the bars on the right have taken up the slack.

I've known the Malamute Saloon since I was underage, sneaking in with a group of friends and sometimes getting a drink before Gustave spotted me and kicked me out. That old pirate didn't bother to card me. After the first time, he knew when my birthday was. When I walked into that bar on my 21st birthday, he shook my hand and bought me a drink, so my first legal drink was on the house. Maybe Gustave's practically giving that bar to Renaldo completed some kind of cosmic circle.

When you walk into a Fourth Avenue bar, you have to pause for a moment while your lungs get used to the sweat and alcohol in the atmosphere and your ears go numb. The bar itself was next to the door, on the right side. Stools were packed tight around a gleaming wooden museum piece, three feet wide and forty feet long, with six bartenders in white shirts, sleeves rolled up, working like machines on an assembly line.

It's hard to concentrate on the bar because immediately beside it is a stage with a Western band. Two amplified guitars, a bass fiddle, and a set of drums were shaking the rafters with "Railroad, Steamboat, River and Canal." The band was dressed Western: fancy shirts, jeans, and cowboy boots, lots of hair, beards and mustaches, but if I was going to look for their steeds in the parking lot, I wouldn't look for horses. I'd look for outlaw motorcycles.

The rest of the room was twilit, the size of a tennis court, with tables all around the walls. Every table had a dozen beer bottles on it and one person on guard; the other two hundred people were dancing.

Don't picture a ballroom. Alaskans live hard, and they party hearty. Picture a Western hoedown with a bad case of Saturday Night Fever. The floor was shaking, the tables bouncing, and the beer sloshing, all to the general beat of "Railroad." Most of the dancers were Eskimos or Indians from the villages, where they live very straight, proper, and sober lives. They were making up for that now with sheer exuberance.

Several patrons were young servicemen from the military bases. They stared in open-mouthed disbelief. The rest were escapees from Somerset Maugham novels with a northern twist.

There were no vacant stools at the bar, but I squeezed in to stand between two guys who had their backs to each other. The one on my right was a cop I knew from a Yupik village, and he was making time with a pretty little girl from Alaska's southeastern panhandle. She had the special grace that proclaimed her tribe Tlingit or Haida. The guy on my left was a *gussak* pilot from Aniak, enthralling a wide-eyed blonde schoolteacher-type with tales of derring-do.

The bartenders were opening beers as fast as they could move and stacking them on trays to be whisked away by waitresses. Renaldo was in the center of the fray, standing head and shoulders above the rest, opening beers at a rate of one per second and sporting the six-inch handlebar mustache that had become his trademark. When I saw that he was still healthy, I felt a release from a subliminal tension, as though I'd been figuratively holding my breath since his call.

As always, Renaldo appeared to have a perfect suntan in spite of having spent the winter in Seattle and Anchorage, but the tan didn't come from a parlor; it was in his genes. I should tell you that his last name is Rodriguez, and the Latin influence is strong. His people came from south of the border, a long ways south: Argentina, where his father had been a functionary in the Peron government.

Argentina was a mess, but for those at the top, life was affluent and good. However, there was disturbing handwriting on the wall. Renaldo's mother was a gringa from Des Moines, Iowa, and when she was heavy with child she made the voyage by steamship and train to her mother's home, specifically so that Renaldo would have undisputed dual citizenship.

He was born in the Mercy Hospital, now usually called Des Moines General. His mother whisked him back to Argentina, where he developed the social skills appropriate to the Spanish court and acquired his taste for riches. The handwriting on the walls got frantic; the walls came crashing down. Peron went into exile, his inner court scattered, and Renaldo ended up rooming with me at a college in Iowa.

He doesn't talk much about those early years, and I've never grilled him. That's fair enough. He's never asked me to explain my English, Irish, Scots mix, and I couldn't do it if he asked.

Renaldo was glancing at the door every couple of minutes, and when he saw me he jerked his head toward the back of the room. I worked my way around the dancers, trying not to get stepped on. Happy, sweating couples would dart out of the pack, grab beer bottles, chug-a-lug, and charge back into the mob. You didn't want to get between a dancer and his beer. Renaldo worked around the other side of the room, and we met at his little cubbyhole office. He closed the door and that helped some. The floor was still shaking, the walls vibrating. The band segued to "Jeremiah Was a Bullfrog," but at least we could hear ourselves shout.

Chapter 3

$\mathcal{R}$enaldo and I never waste time on small talk and greetings; we don't need that. Others may find it hard to understand our relationship. When we talk to each other, a listener would think we were enemies, precisely because we are so solid that we don't have to be nice. When Renaldo called, I was on the next airplane—almost. When the ball is in his court, he does the same, and I'll stake my life on that.

So as usual, Renaldo got right to the point. He gestured me toward a chair, but he was pacing in front of the desk, three steps to the wall and three steps back, stepping over my feet on each pass.

"Last night I was doing the weekly accounting and it was looking pretty good. Forget all that bookkeeping crap we learned in college. This is a cash economy, and I do it all with paper sacks. I had filled up the sack for utilities, and the sack for payroll, and just finished counting thirty thousand into the sack for the next booze order. There was still a good pile of bills on the desk, and I was thinking there would finally be a payday for me."

He stopped pacing, sat down behind the desk, and put his feet on the blotter. He had a little blob of chewing gum stuck to the bottom of one highly polished oxford, maybe the first defect I'd ever seen in Renaldo's haberdashery. He continued.

"It was a little after 3:30 in the morning. The band quits at 2:00; the rest of the help, except for one bartender, leaves at 3:00. There were just a few customers left, mostly sleeping on the tables, maybe a couple curled up on the floor, and I was sitting here with the office door open, watching the front door and doing my Silas Marner act."

Renaldo was too keyed up to sit with his feet up. He slammed them down, leaned over the desk, and supported his chin in hands, elbows on the blotter.

"This guy stomps in the front door, walking real straight and sober, wearing a jacket and tie with a 1950s-style felt hat, looking like Ed Asner.

He marched straight into the office like he knew where he was going, plopped his own paper sack on the desk, and just looked at me.

"'What's that for?' I asked him. 'That's for the insurance payment,' he tells me. 'Just put five thousand in it.' 'I don't want insurance,' I told him. I'm looking at the bills still on the desk, and he's doing the same thing, and it looked like five thousand was about how much was left."

"'Sure you want insurance,' he says. 'It prevents accidents, muggings, maybe a fire. It ain't healthy to run a business without insurance.' I lost my cool. I've been waiting a month for a payday, and damned if I was going to give it to him. I grabbed this pool stick, and I guess all the worries and frustrations of the last month came out. Next thing I knew, I was pounding him on the head and shoulders and chasing him right out the front door."

Renaldo had leaned back and grabbed a cue stick that was standing in the corner. He was holding it by the small end, and for a second it looked like he was going to give me a demonstration of how to use it.

"So, you think maybe he'll be back?" I asked.

"Yeah, I think so. The way he walked right in here like he owned the joint, I think he was on a regular monthly route."

"Well, at least now we know why Gustave sold the bar." That was an unkind dig, but I couldn't help it. Renaldo didn't notice. I tried a more cooperative remark.

"With a little luck, we may not have to wait a month for him to come back."

"No kidding, Sherlock? Why else would I tolerate your ugly mug in my classy bar?"

We left it at that. There was no need to discuss a plan because we both understood what was going to happen next. I dodged my way past the dancers and wandered out the front door. When I glanced back, Renaldo was already behind the bar, opening beers.

I made it, dodging and squeezing, half a block toward C Street where the bars taper off, when I was suddenly surrounded by four young Native guys in National Guard uniforms. I instinctively jerked into a boxing stance, ready to defend myself, but these guys were all smiles, clapping me on the back and shaking both my hands at once. We were outside the Silver Dollar bar, and they were carrying me inside, my toes just touching the sidewalk.

A jukebox was blaring flat out, distorting on the high notes, and somewhere a woofer cone was torn and rattling, but no one was listening to the music. I didn't even notice what was playing. Everyone was shouting to be heard over the music.

My captors sat me down at a table, one of them stole extra chairs, another busted through the crowd to the bar and came back carrying five open Budweisers. I was struggling to place them: nice looking, clean-cut young Eskimo boys, obviously Yupik. They helped me out. They were from Togiak and I had flown them to a National Guard function in Bethel. They were reliving the flight, and the way they told it, it must have been through a hurricane with lightning striking the airplane every couple of minutes.

I took a few sips of the beer, but it was dangerous, because my back was being slapped pretty often. No doubt I flew them across the Kilbuck Mountains, probably half on instruments, and probably routine; at least I had no memory of the flight. They remembered it, moment by moment and lightning flash by lightning flash, apparently fearing for their lives. According to them, I was the greatest pilot since Noel Wien started his airline.

I got half my beer down before they finished theirs. I fought my way to the bar, bought four more Budweisers, shook their hands, clapped their backs, and fled. I made it clear across D Street before I was accosted again. Six Eskimo women were standing indecisively outside the Side Street Bar, thirty feet down D from Fourth Avenue. One of them screamed "Alex!" and charged me.

I was thoroughly hugged. She swiped three feet of straight black hair out of her eyes and raised a very boozy, flat, round Eskimo face for a kiss. I kissed her, not really such an onerous task, and her friends were watching, so it was the gentlemanly thing to do. I probably ingested more alcohol from her breath than I had from the Budweiser.

Maggie was the granddaughter of one of the truly legendary early Bethel pilots. I'd known her since she was a little girl kicking through the dusty streets in Bethel. Now she was a not-so-little girl, kicking around the streets of Anchorage and looking more like forty than her actual age of about twenty. I pressed a twenty-dollar bill into her hand. She pecked my cheek, skipped back to her friends, and they all swooped down the stairs into the Side Street.

My destination on the corner of C Street was the Friendly Loan Co. It's a pawn shop and a veritable supermarket of guns and hardware. I had my .357 magnum Smith and Wesson Patrolman in my jacket pocket, which was legal because I had my private detective badge in my shirt pocket. In Alaska, you can carry anything you want, a submachine gun, I suppose, so long as it's showing. It just takes a permit to carry it concealed.

My problem was that the pistol was loaded, literally, for bear. Those .357 magnum rounds have a way of going through several things before they stop, and just in case I did have to fire the gun in the city, I wanted a box of soft-nosed .38s. When I set the gun on the counter, old Arkyl lit right up, smiling his toothless grin. He whipped out a fifty-dollar bill and offered it to me.

When I snatched the gun away from him and explained my need for a box of .38s, he was still smiling. He should have been; he charged me exactly twice what they were worth. I dumped the .357 rounds on the counter, and then scooped them into my jacket pocket just before Arkyl reached for them. I reloaded with the .38s, same caliber but half as long, shoved the gun back in the right jacket pocket, and checked to be sure I still had my wallet when I stepped back into the street.

I really didn't want any more encounters, so I wandered down the hill on C Street toward the railroad yards and strolled toward the higher-lettered streets on the deserted Third Avenue behind the post office and the parking lots. Before the earthquake, there was a terrace on the north side of Fourth with bars, a theater, and businesses, and another row of businesses below them on Third. After the quake, they were all one jumble, and the area has remained a parking lot since the debris was cleared.

The '64 Alaska earthquake was a good one. I've heard eight-point-six on the Richter scale, one of the strongest ever recorded, and it wasn't the usual one-jolt quake. That baby kept on rocking and rolling for over five minutes. In the same way that most Americans can tell you where they were when Kennedy was shot, Alaskans can tell you where they were during the earthquake. I rode it out in a parking lot on Fifth Avenue. Cars were jumping around the lot, bouncing on their springs, banging together, and I was trying not to get crushed.

Fifth Avenue and the sidewalks were running in waves like the ocean, and I knew it was serious when the whole front of the five-story Penney's department store sloughed off and buried the sidewalk. During that five minutes, the entire Kenai Peninsula tilted, so the town of Portage and the Seward Highway were underwater, and Cordova, on the other side, had docks that were suddenly half a mile from the bay.

I guess the most damage was actually done by the tidal wave. It wiped out Valdez. Railroad trains in Seward tipped over and rolled two blocks up the hill from the waterfront. But I think the greatest loss of life was in Crescent City, California, where they had plenty of warning that a tidal wave was coming. A bunch of people hurried down to the waterfront to watch the tsunami.

The reason there was so much property damage in Anchorage is a layer of thixotropic clay under the city. Thixotropic things turn from a solid to a liquid when you shake them. The example that affects us most is ketchup. The reason that it will never pour when you first try is that it's a solid, not a liquid, when it stands a while.

The people you see in coffee shops shaking the bottle, preferably with the cap still on, are scientifically correct. Shaken enough, the thixotropic ketchup will turn to liquid and will pour. The clay under Anchorage did the same thing. Wherever it reached the surface, like on a bluff or along the ritzy Turnagain Arm area, it turned to liquid and ran out from under the buildings. It wasn't that the buildings weren't strong enough to withstand the earthquake. When the ground ran out from under them, they came down.

Anyhow, Third Avenue was peaceful that night, just a parking lot with a few cars and a grass bluff coming down from Fourth Avenue. I could hear the music, but it wasn't rattling my head, so I could look down on the railroad yards, hear a diesel switch engine working, and watch a flight of C-130s lift off from Elmendorf Air Force Base on the next hill.

I wavered outside the Westward Hotel, remembering the escargot in the Chart Room, waffled outside The Wood Shed, thinking of the Roquefort dressing that demands martinis, but continued on up Third Avenue to Elevation 92. That's a world-class restaurant, named for its height above sea level, but it offered a view across Cook Inlet, all the way to Mt. Denali.

Anchorage has more than its share of very fine restaurants, and that's not just the little boy from the bush talking. For the very best in price-is-no-object dining, you can't beat Anchorage, and Elevation 92 was the crème-de-la-crème. I was enthroned in a glass wonderland, pampered, tantalized, and stuffed. An hour later, I floated back toward Renaldo's bar on a happy cloud of garlic butter, fresh clams, and Roquefort that they import daily from heaven.

I climbed up G Street, past the Westward Hotel to a subdued and civilized, or at least deserted, portion of Fourth Avenue. The theater was showing its last movie of the night, so no one was outside. Woolworths was closed, Zales Jewelry, Seidenverg, and Kays Men's Shop, and so on, all dark and quiet. Stewart's Photo, where Ivan and Ora have served Anchorage forever, was closed, but I stopped to admire the rock collection in the window.

I first met Ivan and Ora Stewart many years ago when I flew them up to Jade Mountain on the Kobuk River to do some prospecting. Once you meet them, they are friends for life. Their other attention-grabbing gimmick, besides the rock collection, was their pet reindeer that got very popular around Christmas time but left a trail of little black pellets wherever he walked.

The Five-Fifteen Club was open, but you had to take the neon sign's word for that. The sidewalk wasn't shaking and the walls weren't vibrating.

The public library made a gothic silhouette across the street, with a special light illuminating the stone sculpture on the lawn. The stone sculpture was just that, a stone, and there was quite a public furor when the city paid the artist several thousand dollars for it, but maybe it was an artistic stone.

By that time, the cacophony beyond E Street was starting to suck me in, like a whirlpool of light and music. I caressed the pistol in my pocket. To understand my relationship with the pistol, you have to know my father, and my relationship with him.

Dad was Scotch and English, raised on a ranch in the southern Idaho desert, and he was into manly things. For instance, one of his sports was relay horse racing. That consisted of riding four horses in turn, two in each direction over a prescribed course, changing horses at each end of the track. Dad was unbeatable, because he could ride one horse at a dead run past the waiting one, reach out and grab the saddle horn with one hand, and swing himself across into the other saddle.

His other sport was football, and he played the line, usually right tackle. When I came along, with half my genes from mother's Irish, I never measured up to Dad's expectations. I played football as a halfback in high school, well enough for a scholarship to Iowa where I played quarterback, but Dad thought the backfield was sissy stuff. All the guys in the backfield had to do was just not drop the ball and walk through the alleys that Dad opened up in the opposing lines.

I was getting to be as tall as Dad, but only half as wide and half as thick. He would pull into the yard with three one-hundred-pound sacks of grain in the back of a pickup. He would grab two of the sacks by the ears, one in each hand, and walk out to the granary with them while I struggled behind him with the remaining sack on my shoulder.

I was fourteen when Dad made one more attempt to teach me a manly art. He took me down into the basement where he had rigged up a target in front of a mattress. He unwrapped a Hi-Standard .22 caliber target pistol and snapped off nine shots, all of them in the center of the bull's eye. Then he tossed the pistol to me and went back upstairs.

My first nine shots were all on the mattress, but I kept at it, and little by little discovered to my great delight, and eventually to Dad's, that I could shoot. Dad would bring home cronies to sit on the cellar stairs and drink beer while they watched "his boy" put box after box of .22 shells all through the same hole in the center of the bull's eye. That was my first taste of paternal approval. I ate it up, and kept practicing.

When I went to the police academy to qualify for my concealed weapon permit, I used my .357, snapped off six shots in three seconds, and put the gun away. The instructor was shaking his head, thinking I had missed the target because he didn't see any holes. He did a double take when he found all six holes centered in the bull's eye in a cluster you could cover with a silver dollar.

Next to airplanes, I guess a lot of my identity was wrapped up in that pistol, and caressing it was a little like having Dad there in my corner. I crossed E Street, passed the open doors of the Union Club that spewed out "Proud Mary"; passed the Four Aces bar, ("Sweet Dreams, Baby"); passed Eric Clapton's "Cocaine" from the Paradise Club, and ducked into Renaldo's Malamute, where the band was blaring a Lynyrd Skynrd number, bastardized to "Sweet Home Alaska."

Chapter 4

Two o'clock came and the band left. Customers followed as if the band had been pied pipers. Someone put money in the jukebox, and Elvis warned us about his Blue Suede Shoes, but the party was over. By 2:30, the waitresses were mostly just picking up empties and wiping tables. By 3:00, there was just one bartender behind the polished mahogany bar and maybe a dozen customers, most of them sprawled across now clean tables.

I took a table that put me near the door, with a chunk of solid log wall beyond the door. The logs were there for effect: it was actually a cement-block building, but the logs were real and would stop a bullet. Renaldo emptied five of the six cash registers into a beer box and carried his loot back to the office. He left the door open, so I could see him back there counting. Most of the bills I'd seen were ones and fives, so if he needed thirty thousand for the next booze order, it was going to take him a while.

A fairly sober, fortyish Eskimo woman wearing a housedress stomped in. She set her feet firmly in a Sumo stance, hands on generous hips, and surveyed the bar with an angry scowl. She suddenly charged to a rear table, grabbed its occupant by the hair, and marched him out. That must have stirred some consciences, because three more patrons staggered out right after them.

The bartender was stacking boxes of empty bottles, whistling along with Elvis to "Hound Dog." The street, visible through the plate glass window beside me, and through the open glass door, was mostly empty, except for taxicabs and the stragglers trying to climb into them.

Two heavies stomped in, and these were not Ed Asner types. These were straight from *The Godfather*. They were dressed like Washington state loggers on Sunday, sports jackets over jeans with logging boots. Both were wearing holstered pistols long enough to show below their jackets. I did not think they were the liquor commission.

"Hold it right there," I said. "The bar is closed."

They both spun toward me and the ugliest one grabbed for his gun. Maybe it was a reflex action, or maybe my table was dark enough that they couldn't see the pistol in my hand. There's something about drawing a gun that puts time into slow motion. He flicked back his jacket, grabbed the gun butt, and was pulling eight inches of barrel out of his holster. I let him get it most of the way out before I shot it out of his hand. Time switched back to normal. He jerked his hand up and stuck bloody fingers into his mouth.

"Next?" I invited, but they pivoted around and disappeared out the door.

Renaldo came bouncing out from the office. "Hey, what's the idea of shooting up my bar?"

"Sorry, I guess I panicked."

"Don't you know that violence begets violence?" he demanded. "Now you've escalated this into a shooting war. Couldn't you just slap them around a little?"

"I don't think those guys were much into slapping." I walked over and retrieved the hog leg from the floor behind the door. It was a .44 magnum revolver, capable of winning the west, and maybe the north, too. I handed it to Renaldo, and he held it by the butt between two fingers, as if he was holding up a dead rat by the tail.

"What am I supposed to do with this?"

"I don't know, hold it for ransom maybe." I sat back down at my table; Renaldo stalked indignantly back to his office, still holding the gun as if it were diseased. The last two patrons who had been sleeping across the tables roused themselves and staggered out. I guess Renaldo had a point. Guns seemed to be bad for business.

The bartender finished stacking, stopped whistling, and carried the last cash drawer back to the office. He came out counting a roll of bills and escaped out the front door. Renaldo got up from his desk and stuffed brown paper bags, like kid's lunch sacks, into a wall safe and stuck the final cash drawer in on top of them. He came out of the office, yawning and stretching.

"Ready for some dinner?" he asked.

"Nah, I may never eat again. I stocked up on clams at Elevation 92."

Renaldo hiked up a jacket sleeve to consult a gold Bulova that nestled next to a gold cufflink on an immaculate white cuff. "They're closed now, but maybe Clinkerdagger's has some burnt cream left. Sure you don't want to come?"

"Thanks, but I think this is a good place for me to stay right now."

"Suit yourself." Renaldo strolled out, closed the glass door, and turned to lock it. I waved him away. I had a feeling that getting that door open fast might be real important in the next few hours. Renaldo disappeared toward E Street, and a couple of minutes later I heard a car start in the alley behind the bar. It sounded to me like a Porsche, or maybe a Jaguar. It had a resonance like a cat purring, but a very large and virile cat.

I half felt my way through the semi-darkness to check the back door. It was a solid steel affair, suitable for Fort Knox, locked with sliding bolts like a screen door, except the bolts were thicker than my fingers. I slid the bolts and the door opened easily. The alley out back was dark and deserted. The back of the bar, and in fact the whole alley side, was concrete blocks, probably safe against anything short of a howitzer. I slid the bolts closed and went back to my seat by the front door.

A city paddy wagon, red lights flashing, inched down the street. Two cops were gathering up bodies off the curb and out of the doorways and tossing them in the back of the wagon. In those days, they would dump the bodies in the drunk tank until morning, probably dirtier and less comfortable than the street, but maybe safer, certainly preferable in winter. They don't do that anymore. The American Civil Liberties people stopped all that because being drunk in public is not a crime in Alaska.

Nowadays the drunks just lie where they fall, freeze to death in winter, get robbed or murdered in summer, but their civil rights are not violated. It's like a warped take on Eskimo tradition: they don't tell each other what to do. I guess that worked for a few thousand years, but not so well since alcohol entered the picture. For instance, during one of Bethel's wet periods, a friend of mine was struggling homeward with his wife and sister-in-law who had come in from a village. They had soaked up beer in the Old Pool Hall until it closed around three in the morning. Temperature was twenty below, the three of them hold-ing each other up and staggering toward their cabin. They had a quarter of a mile left to go when the sister decided she wanted to take a nap. She flopped down in the snow beside the road and commenced to snore. My friend and his wife wove their way on home; the sister had a right to do what she wished to do, by custom they had no right to interfere, and by drinking so much they had lost sight of the overwhelming reasons to forget custom and interfere.

They went back in the morning to see if she had made it. She hadn't. She was frozen driftwood-log solid. Her death was ruled accidental.

After the red light stopped bouncing off the walls, the most excitement was the occasional hum when one of the coolers ran for a while. I sat there for what seemed like an hour, alternately wishing that I had invited Connie to come into town with me and wondering how Bushmaster was going to pay their insurance premium next month.

Connie was the nicer of the two thoughts, so I spent more time on her. She's a divorcée who fled all the way from central Missouri to Bethel and went to work in the district attorney's office. She wears heels, hose, and makeup, all very unusual and very welcome in Bethel. With auburn, shoulder-length hair and sparkling blue eyes, she was a nice subject for thoughts.

A black sedan whipped around the corner and screeched to a stop in the taxi zone out front. Funny how you can tell when the driver is sober, and that made it stand out from anything I'd seen lately. I stood behind the frame at the side of the glass door and peeked out, ready to hit the floor in case the bar was going to get raked with machine guns. There were two guys in the front seat, I think the same cowboys who were in earlier. The passenger bent over, and when he sat up, he had a bottle in his hand and was lighting the wick on a Molotov cocktail.

A Molotov cocktail is an old-fashioned do-it-yourself kind of weapon; it's a bottle full of gasoline with a rag wick stuffed in the top. The wick keeps the gasoline in, but enough fumes escape to make the wick burn really well, and when the bottle spills or breaks you have an instant conflagration.

The guy tossed the bottle in a nice high arc toward the glass door. I jerked the door open and caught the bottle; it was a Budweiser, and getting hot. I tossed it right back to him, only the car was peeling away and the bottle went in the open back window. I caught a glimpse of both guys turned around in their seats. The car careened across the street and slammed into a light pole. The next instant, there was a muffled "poof" sound and flames belched out of all the car windows. I closed the door.

I'm not really heartless enough to let two guys burn to death, even Luca Brasi types, but it was already too late. They were crispy critters right from the *poof.* The car was a raging torch, but sitting alone in the street not threatening anything else, so I just watched. In five minutes, two police cruisers came screaming up and a minute later the whole street was filled with fire trucks, hoses crisscrossing everywhere, and men in yellow slickers running back and forth. Some of the trucks were hinged in the middle, with extendible ladders looking like they might go up several hundred feet.

When the fire trucks untangled the hoses and left, the car was a steaming hulk with two ambulance drivers extracting bundles from the front seat. I sure didn't envy those guys. The ambulance pulled away with no siren. A tow truck hooked onto the car and raised the front bumper, dragging the car on two flat rear tires with the rims shooting sparks. The final cop car followed the wrecker, red lights flashing. They turned the corner at C Street, and tranquility settled in. I heard a car park behind the bar and braced for the explosion, but a minute later Renaldo sauntered in the front door.

"Well, any excitement?" he asked.

"Nah, we're wasting our time here. If Clinkerdagger's is still open, I could use a drink, but I won't be eating burnt cream any time soon." There was no point filling Renaldo in on the details. The show was over, so why spoil his evening?

We grabbed stools at the bar in Clinkerdagger's, surrounded by more old-world memorabilia on the walls than most museums have. I ordered the calamari appetizer, deep-fried with tartar sauce on the side, and we finally had time to talk. Mostly, Renaldo could not understand why I hadn't married Connie and didn't quite believe that it was her choice, not mine. Renaldo was always in the position of turning down women and didn't understand that it could be the other way around.

Connie's ex was a long-haul truck driver who turned out to have a girl in every town. She liked me well enough, but she wanted a man who was home at 5:30 every evening. My whereabouts at 5:30 in the evening depended entirely on Vicki's phone calls, and Connie wasn't ready for that.

By 5:30 in the morning, even Clinkerdagger's was closing, lights coming on and vacuum cleaners going to work on the labyrinth of memorabilia that decorated their dining area. By that time, I had inhaled half a bottle of Captain Morgan's rum in Coke. I could have ordered that in Renaldo's bar, but I hadn't, because I would have been served a glass of Bacardi, lightly colored with dishwater. There is a good reason why Fourth Avenue drinkers stick to bottled beer.

It was daylight, although the sun wasn't up yet. In Alaska, the sun goes sideways, parallel to the horizon, and slides over gradually instead of coming straight up and going straight down the way it does at lower latitudes. In winter it does its teasing, and any rising that it's going to do, in the south. By late spring it was making its prolonged sunrise colors several degrees north of west. It would be un-Alaskan of me to say that it was cold, but it was definitely bracing, hovering below fifty degrees until the sun peeked over, and would leap into the seventies when that red ball finally appeared. It was also quiet, which I found disconcerting in the middle of the city.

Renaldo wheeled his Alfa Romeo (it turned out to be the Spider model, a lipstick-red convertible with black leather seats that you wanted to make love to) into the parking lot at the Sheffield House hotel, dumped me off, and sped away. He was staying at the Eagle House himself; that's a house-sharing arrangement by a bunch of professional men, with no overnight guests allowed.

There were other options. The Captain Cook Hotel, two more blocks down Fifth, was built by Wally Hickel, an ex-governor. It was classy but dark, with the windows in the rooms permanently sealed. I always felt as if you needed a necktie to go in there. The old Anchorage Westward was two blocks away on Third, emphasis on the old, but constantly refurbished. It changed so often that I could never find my way around in there. The Sheraton has wonderful restaurants but was way down on Seventh Avenue, too far from the action, and filled with tourists.

The Sheffield House belonged to Bill Sheffield, another ex-governor, and was the choice of Bush types, partly because it's bright and cheerful, partly because every room has a balcony and sliding glass doors so you never feel claustrophobic. I was really impressed by the Philippine mahogany pillars in the coffee shop until I noticed that they were contact paper over concrete. Anyhow, Bush types like to stick together, and the Sheffield House had become our Anchorage headquarters.

I asked for, and got, room 1107. That's in the middle of the north, Mt. Denali, side, and some architectural anomaly had made it much larger than most of the hotel's rooms. I took my key and turned toward the elevator. The shout was déjà vu all over again, "Alex!" just like on D Street. Maggie bounded out of the twenty-four-hour coffee shop and linked arms with me. That was not a coincidence. She knew I'd be staying there, so she had been waiting. No one paid the least attention, and we proceeded to the elevators.

Maggie squeezed my arm not unlike Anna had squeezed my finger, until we got into the room. She let out a whoop and started shedding clothes while she headed for the bathroom. She left a trail: blouse, shoes, skirt, panties. No bra, no socks. I reloaded the pistol, stuck it into a drawer on the nightstand, and hung my jacket in the closet. It occurred to me that I hadn't packed a bag, so I was going to have to buy some clothes.

The bathroom door was open and I had an urgent call, so I wandered in. The shower curtain was closed, a regular waterfall going on behind it, and steam billowing over, under, and past it. I did what I had to do, went back to the main room, and opened the drapes. The sun was coming up but still hadn't topped the mountains. It made a pastel, rose-and-orange curtain behind a black silhouette of the Chugach Range. I cracked the sliding glass door to the balcony to let some air in, because there were serious alcohol fumes inside: some of mine, lots of Maggie's. I stripped to shorts and crawled into what had just become my half of the king-sized bed.

Maggie came out of the shower groping for a towel. Naked, she still looked like a teenager, lean and willowy, with champagne-glass-sized breasts and a flat little belly. She wiped her eyes, then stripped water out of her hair for a while and used the towel to make a turban. She grabbed another towel and finished the drying job. The shower had done wonders for her, and I take back that crack I made earlier about her looking forty years old; twenty-one, tops, and that's for legal reasons.

If you haven't spent some time with the Eskimos, you might be getting the wrong idea here. The way Maggie strutted out of the shower naked and rubbed herself down, I could understand that idea, but forget it. Maggie was living on the Eskimo survival technique of sharing. I had a bed and a shower; she needed same, so we shared them. Any friend coming in from the Bush meant a place to stay for a few days.

That was not a one-sided situation. Now and again, I'll be stuck overnight in a village, and if not Maggie, then one of her cousins will provide bed and board and in general treat me like royalty.

From the way Maggie attacked that shower, I guessed it had been a while since the sharing had been good, and her snoring in three seconds in her half of the bed, still wearing her towel turban, confirmed that she needed the bed, too. I don't mean to imply that Maggie was virginal, probably far from it, but that was in another context. In this context, I was a friend; maybe she thought of me as an uncle. It would never occur to Maggie that I might take advantage of the situation, so I didn't let it occur to me, either. I watched the rising sun turn Mt. Denali from strawberry ice cream into a golden tower. That sounds as if Denali is by itself, and it isn't. It's in the solid line of the Alaska Range, and if you ignore the political boundaries, those mountains reach all the way from Mexico to the Aleutian Chain: only the names change. It's just that Denali sticks up another seven thousand feet above all of the others. I pretended to count mountain sheep, got used to the subliminal music of Maggie's breathing, a soloist working against the choral background of the city awakening, and went to sleep.

Chapter 5

*M*eanwhile, in another time and place...

Jossef was raised in Odessa, which is Russia's answer to the French Riviera, with a generous dollop of Las Vegas thrown in. The subject of school seldom came up, so he spent his youth wandering the boardwalks along sunny golden beaches. At age twelve, he was fox-faced. His nose, protruding under a thatch of black straw, as well as his hands and feet, had grown faster than the rest of him. He was tall, and skinny for his age, but fast, very fast. He watched yachts and small boats that patrolled the Black Sea coast, but he wore running shoes and never missed a chance to make a hasty exit with any beach bag that an unwary bather left unattended.

His father was listed on the state rolls as a factory worker, and there may have been a factory that recognized him, but his real business was extortion and the black market. The Soviet economy was in such a shambles that earning an honest living was out of the question, or at least Jossef didn't know anyone who tried.

Jossef's father could have been called barrel chested, but his build and posture bore such a striking resemblance to the Russian bear that a very young Jossef was confused and thought that his father was the symbol of Russia.

During his thirteenth year, Jossef took on the daily task of trading stolen goods and black market items for the best of meats and vegetables, his father handling the deals that kept his mother in the jewels and furs she loved, and his father driving a Zil sedan.

Jossef's mother held her patrician, if aging, head high, and never missed a chance to mention that she was "of the French blood." She tinted her graying brown hair red and was always carefully permed, made up, and usually wearing jewels, but Jossef never knew of her going out anywhere.

33

She spent most of her time in front of a mirror, often trying to rub out the encroaching wrinkles with her finger. Jossef barely noticed her. Women were of no consequence in his world, and words like "love" or "affection" were never uttered in their household.

It was a shipment of Kalashnikov rifles, stolen, or more accurately, handed over by bribable army officials, that brought Jossef's idyllic world crashing down. His father had sold the rifles to a South American fruit consortium and paid the army officials. A rival had sold the same rifles to an archeological research company in Iran and also paid the officials. When the rival black marketeer discovered that the rifles were missing, he lost his sense of humor and uttered the ugly word *hit*.

Jossef's mother started packing early that afternoon. His father went out as usual, but instead of coming home after midnight, reeking of vodka and singing at the top of his lungs, he was home at 9:30 carrying sacks of gold and diamonds. Mother stashed diamonds in the luggage wherever she could hide them, filling up toothpaste tubes and hollow heels on shoes. She packed more books than Jossef had ever seen; he had no idea where she had found them. The middles of the books were cut out and consigned to the fireplace, the hollows filled with diamonds.

Jossef and his father hid the gold in household furniture that his father's best and most trusted friend would ship to them. That was the night that Jossef found out he was Jewish, whatever that meant, and the family was emigrating to Israel. Before the morning sun lit the Ukraine, the little family was in a railroad carriage, making their pilgrimage.

After the freewheeling thrills of Odessa, life on the kibbutz was impossibly dull for Jossef. He worked in the fields and developed calluses, but the family was comfortable, doling out diamonds as necessary. Even though the friend never shipped the furniture, Jossef's father seemed to be retired. Jossef's mother wore her jewels and furs, perspiring in the privacy of their flat, and was content.

When his eighteenth birthday loomed, Jossef discovered that being Jewish meant being drafted into the Israeli Navy. That was a relief after the kibbutz, and he began to find ways to supplement his stipend, running gambling games and supplying the occasional prostitute. He learned hand-to-hand combat, at which he was very good because he had no conscience or pity. He learned weapons, at which he was very good because he saw their implication for his future.

By age twenty-four, he was approaching six feet tall, wearing long hair, a black mustache, caterpillar eyebrows, and a permanent sneer. He now roamed the streets of Frankfurt, Germany, attaching himself to ever-more prestigious and nefarious mobs. He was happy, with money to burn, required only to ambush and kill an occasional rival, or break knees when someone couldn't pay his debts. He learned the management aspects of the sex trade and the bountiful profits that accrued therefrom, at least to the overlords. The protection racket was a cinch. Anyone who didn't pay disappeared, and the businesses passed to the mob.

Occasionally, an enforcer was blown away by a shotgun, but they were the slow ones. Jossef always shot first, sometimes before the victim had even heard of the racket. Frankfurt was even better than Odessa, until a bigger fish showed up from Berlin. A territorial struggle ensued; the opponents were armed soldiers instead of unarmed shopkeepers, and the word *hit* was bandied about.

With the wisdom learned at his father's knee, Jossef caught a night train back to Odessa. Things were more organized in Odessa than Jossef remembered. All of the old occupations were still available, but everyone seemed to be working for someone higher up, in a pyramid that descended directly from the Kremlin. He was making contacts, currying favor, and squirming back into the business when the Western world descended on him.

In the 1970s, the West, perhaps trying to atone for its part in the Holocaust, was putting tremendous pressure on Russia to allow Jews to emigrate. Russia obliged by sweeping hordes of undesirables off their streets, emptying their jails and mental hospitals, and cleaning up seedy areas of towns. Jossef was caught in the net. He found himself standing on a street corner in Brighton Beach, Brooklyn, New York, along with forty thousand other Russian immigrants.

Fearful of law enforcement in a strange country, he got a legitimate job in a Russian-owned furniture factory and was amazed to earn a wage that would actually sustain him. With his professional feel for business, he quickly discovered that the furniture they shipped was full of cocaine. This was followed by the discovery of just how wealthy an ordinary factory worker could become. He made a lateral transfer from his glue gun and mallet to a .45 in a shoulder holster and a set of brass knuckles in a suit coat pocket.

When he bought his Datsun 480-Z, Jossef fondly remembered his father's Zil and felt that he had finally grown up. The passenger seat in the Datsun attracted a steady stream of flashy women sporting blonde hair with variously colored roots. They reminded him of his mother with their passions for jewelry and furs. Their other passions were a pleasant surprise, until the day that he found Denise parked in the Datsun, intriguing nylons crossed under short skirt and sweater threads stretched to a scream.

Denise was different from the other girls in that her father was a capo in the Russian mob, and she didn't dive for his zipper whenever he parked. That got Jossef's attention. She was unabashedly brunette, almost five-foot ten, which is statuesque by Russian standards, and usually scowling, but she showed no intention of relinquishing the seat. Her skirts got ever shorter, nylons longer, sweaters tighter, and she did love furs and jewelry, but she seemed to have a mild distaste for Jossef himself and no interest at all in his zipper.

The weight of her mother's tongue, her father's cold stares, and thousands of years of tradition had conspired to force Denise to find a husband. She picked Jossef as the least objectionable candidate, but the thought of marriage made her skin crawl.

Denise's father, Big Tony, was ruthless, cruel, vindictive, scheming, and in general reminded Jossef fondly of his own father. Tony began treating Jossef like a son-in-law, which included a transfer from the cocaine-laced furniture business to a little grocery store that imported Russian delicacies. Jossef's duties at the grocery store were to visit the other businesses along the street and collect their monthly payments. The payments were a form of tribute and gratitude to Big Tony for letting them live, and the only ones unhappy with the arrangement were some die-hard Italians who were prejudiced against immigrants.

Jossef and his fellow grocery clerks took the Italians swimming, and kept a Russian fish market busy preparing Sicilian messages. A garment belonging to a recently deceased was wrapped around a fish and sent to the appropriate Italians, conveying to them that the owner now slept with the fishes. Jossef was amazed and delighted with his new country where opportunities were unlimited and any immigrant boy could grow up to be a capo.

He did, however, miss the attentions of the blondes grabbing for his zipper. Denise still wasn't grabbing, and with her in the seat, no one else was either. Jossef began to suspect the answer to an enigma that had always puzzled him. He had never understood why his father, who took his pick of the ladies of Odessa nights, had married his mother.

When the engagement was announced, Big Tony gave Jossef a territory of his own on Avenue Z, reaching all the way from Coney Island Avenue to Ocean Avenue. Jossef recruited several old friends from the Odessa days, and with dependable Russian equipment like Kalashnikov rifles, they set about clearing the Italians out of his new domain.

The wedding was a gala affair at Coney Island, with three live bands and cases of vodka direct from Mother Russia to wash down the caviar. As the man of the hour, second only to Big Tony, Jossef celebrated until his friends carried his inert remains back to his apartment and dumped him on the floor. The blushing bride remained sober and returned to her father's house.

As a married lady, Denise assumed a more proper decorum, no longer tantalizing Jossef in the Datsun. The zipper-grabbing blondes began to trickle back into his car and his apartment. The repatriation of Avenue Z progressed nicely. Italian, Irish, and even Jewish shopkeepers of non-Russian extraction sold their businesses to Russians, sometimes for a dollar, sometimes not. Occasionally, Russians just found the businesses unoccupied and moved in, all of them very grateful and happy to pay tribute to Jossef.

The life of an American businessman suited Jossef well. He turned his attention to larger and more political issues, like the DEA agents, or suspected agents, who sometimes harassed his shopkeepers. Four new immigrants arrived from Russia and were eager to fit into the community. They had American dollars with them and American haircuts, and spoke a brand of Russian that struck Jossef as baby talk. The newcomers immediately wanted to buy drugs from Jossef's hardware and grocery stores.

Feinberg, the grocer, per protocol, asked Jossef's permission to unload a few kilos to one of the friendly new immigrants. Jossef told him to go ahead with the sale, but showed up with a couple of friends to supervise the transaction. When the new man came bustling in with a briefcase full of money, Jossef grabbed the case and his friends stripped the buyer.

They found a tiny transmitter taped to the small of his back and an antenna hanging down inside his pants leg. One of Jossef's friends used brass knuckles to bust the buyer's teeth out of the way, and then used a pair of pliers to pull out his tongue and a pair of scissors to cut it off. That stopped his screaming. The friends bent the buyer over and held him while Jossef inserted the transmitter into the thrashing anal cavity and used a can of beans off the shelf to drive it home.

They dragged the still-conscious buyer out onto the street and used the antenna to tie his neck to a lamppost. Pedestrians on the street minded their own business in typical New York fashion. Jossef took his friends to lunch.

Life could have gone on in that idyllic fashion for a long time, but Jossef's new mother-in-law wanted a grandchild and seemed to think that Jossef should get involved. Big Tony pronounced the decree. Jossef packed up Monica and booted her out of the apartment, fur coats, jewelry, Siamese cats, and all. Tony's friends delivered a defiant Denise to the front door, carried her up the steps, and shoved her inside.

Instead of stripping and lying down as a good wife should, Denise used terms like "scumbag" and "filthy Jewish bastard" and other remarks that Jossef remembered from his childhood on the rare nights when his father had come home unsatisfied.

He had a nostalgic flashback to his early years, standing at the bottom of the big curved staircase in Odessa, listening to those same remarks screamed from his parent's bedroom, along with crashing furniture. He felt a flush of pride, remembering his father's virility.

Jossef had developed an interest in Denise's assets during the weeks she had tantalized him, so he grabbed her sweater and tried to pull it up. She held it down, screaming obscenities right in his face. Russian men do know how to handle their women. Like his father before him, and Big Tony himself, whose wife often sported black eyes and had a permanently broken nose, Jossef started some Russian foreplay.

He grabbed Denise's right breast in a vise grip with his left hand to hold her still, and patiently slapped her face back and forth with his right hand. He ignored her scratching talons, and slapped a little harder with each blow until she crumpled onto the carpet. He removed the impediments, was happy to find that he had indeed married a very sexy lady, and fulfilled his mother-in-law's wish.

Jossef was satisfied, both physically and with having discharged his husbandly duty. When Denise wrapped her torn sweater and buttonless skirt around her and ran screaming out the door, Jossef let her go, not thinking much about it. It certainly never occurred to him that Big Tony would wish his daughter to be treated differently than he himself treated his wife.

It was a shock to Jossef when one of his friends called an hour later and whispered the ugly word: *hit.*

Chapter 6

Jossef had internalized the Boy Scout motto. He was prepared. From under his bed, he grabbed the briefcase that contained clean socks, underwear, and all of his cash. He parked the Datsun at Kennedy International and left the keys in it. Forty minutes later, the Datsun was in a chop shop, and Jossef was on an Eastern Airlines shuttle flight to Miami.

Reluctantly, he shaved off his mustache and trimmed his eyebrows to create a new persona. He explored the situation in Miami by hiring taxis for sightseeing trips and chatting up the drivers for information. Every third taxi he hired was driven by a Russian. At first they were startled when he addressed them in the mother tongue, but he dropped names from Odessa and Brooklyn, omitting only Big Tony from his résumé, and on his third day in town he was introduced to the owner of a taxi company. For a week, he drove a cab, cruised, and tried to learn the town, picking up an occasional fare and earning around forty dollars a shift, while the company checked out his connections back in Odessa and Brooklyn.

At the end of a week, he was given a codebook with words to indicate heroin, coke, crack, pot, four different flavors of sex, poker games, and cockfights. From then on, when his fares expressed a desire, he used the code word, was directed to a rendezvous, and his income leapt to four hundred dollars a day. But Jossef wasn't satisfied. He kept up a steady pressure to learn the hierarchy of the Russian-run side of the town and find out who was in charge.

What he found was eerily reminiscent of the new Odessa. The city was tightly organized, and the men at the top were ex-KGB agents, some who didn't even speak English, others who were highly respected local businessmen at ease in English and Spanish as well. Jossef resumed the old familiar game of working his way up, but he didn't buy a Datsun, and when he wanted a blonde, he paid her asking price.

The break came when he discovered that one of the high rollers, a man named Samson, was from Odessa and remembered Jossef's father. Jossef became a doorman at a strip club, providing protection, coercion where needed, and ensuring that visiting dignitaries enjoyed themselves and found the particular brands of sex and drugs that suited them. He began to understand that the parts useful to him of not only Miami and Brooklyn, but all of America, were organized by the Russians.

His one worry was that Big Tony might drop in for some rest and relaxation, so he was greatly relieved when he heard that Tony had stopped a dozen Italian bullets on the sidewalk in front of his grocery store.

Jossef was aware, from the luxury condos in North Miami Beach and the multimillion dollar mansions on Fisher Island, that the sources of income went far beyond the sex and drugs in the city. It began to make sense when Jossef was invited to accompany Samson on a quick trip to Columbia. Jossef's job was to stand around and look dangerous, and he did that well, but he also listened. In Columbia, he learned that entire shiploads of cocaine were plying the oceans between Guayaquil, Ecuador, and Leningrad, in Russia.

Samson was brokering the deals and laundering the money, millions of dollars per shipload, but that wasn't the thrust of his business. The trip to Columbia was to discuss the purchase of several heavy-lift helicopters from the corrupt and crumbling Russian military, and the names Medellin, Cali, Escobar, and Noriega were bandied about. Jossef was disappointed when he didn't get to go along the following week to Latvia.

He was instead stuck at the club, with the duty of making sure that a couple of visiting capos from Seattle enjoyed themselves and would wake up in their own beds after they passed out. The party had moved to a dungeon where the capos sat bug-eyed, whiffing down cocaine, while they watched bound and gagged women being whipped on stage.

The show was boring because it was all make believe. Jossef was more interested in watching the patrons and figuring out who was who than he was in the show. He recognized the kingpin from Denver, and then was shocked almost out of his seat when he realized that one of the kingpin's bodyguards was one of the phony "Russians," one of the DEA agents who had tried to penetrate Jossef's street in Brooklyn. Two days later, another Russian came into the club, ordered a drink, and watched the strippers. The guy had shaved his beard and had a new suntan, but Jossef was positive that this was another of the infiltrators from Brooklyn.

Samson came back from Latvia looking very pleased with himself. Jossef tried to tell him that the DEA was moving in, expecting orders to take them swimming or perhaps visit a local meat market, but Samson was riding a bubble and refused to worry. Jossef began seeing suspicious characters everywhere. Half the people who came into the club looked like DEA men to him. He realized he was being thoroughly paranoid, but he also knew there were worse things—like being imprisoned or dead. He quietly liquidated his assets and packed his bag. He had arrived in Miami with a paltry two million bucks; the bag was quite a lot heavier when he stashed it under the seat of his secondhand Plymouth.

The day he came to work to find the parking lot full of dark sedans and the Miami police guarding the driveway, Jossef drove right on by, straight to the highway and the airport in Fort Lauderdale. He bought a ticket to Atlanta, changed airlines there, and bought a ticket for Minneapolis. He changed airlines again and shivered in Seattle while he waited for his flight to the one state in the union that wasn't organized. He climbed off an Alaska Airlines 727 in Anchorage, walked straight through the terminal and caught a Wien Airlines 737 to Fairbanks.

In Fairbanks, the taxi drivers were ethnically a bit of almost everything, except Russians. He rented a penthouse suite in the Polaris Building, with a view of the Chena River that wound through town and mountains beyond that reminded him of Russia. He holed up in his aerie, studied the want ads, and plunked down two hundred thousand cash to buy a massage parlor on South Cushman Street at the edge of town.

The massage parlor was a stark rectangle of concrete blocks with no windows, nestled between the Squadron Club taxi-dancing emporium and the Kit Kat Klub strip bar. A parking lot out front could hold twenty cars, usually with several stalls occupied, and taxis cruised through constantly. There seemed to be several women in permanent residence, none of them ever dressed enough to go outside.

Thus established as a legitimate Fairbanks businessman, Jossef joined the Chamber of Commerce and the Elks Lodge. At the end of the month, when a Fairbanks city cop showed up at the massage parlor for a payoff, Jossef paid him and followed him. By the end of the second month, he knew which cops were involved in the protection racket, and that they met in a bar on First Avenue to divide the spoils.

At the end of the third month of his life in Fairbanks, when the last of the courier-cops had arrived at the First Avenue bar and gone into the private gaming room in back, Jossef, disguised as an old man who had been almost asleep over his beer, staggered to his feet. He lurched toward the restroom, still wearing his overcoat and hat. When he passed the gaming room, he stumbled against the door, fell into the room, jerked a Kalashnikov out of his coat and emptied it in four-inch steps all the way around the room. He stood up, surveyed the effects of the Kalashnikov with a touch of national pride, and walked out to confront the cowering bartender. Jossef placed a pile of bills, ten thousand dollars in crisp new hundreds, on the bar.

"There's $500 for every Russian soldier that you saw burst through that door with rifles. If you forget that, well, you saw what the Kalashnikov can do."

By the end of the fourth month, the bagman who made the collection rounds of all the bars and businesses that normally need police protection was an old friend of Jossef's from Brooklyn who spoke fluent Russian but looked like Ed Asner. Yuri was the seventh son of a seventh son, and back in Odessa old women had waited for him to develop magical powers, but all he ever noticed getting from his heritage was the knack of taking orders from everyone around him. When Yuri came to collect the insurance, Jossef handed over the protection money from his massage parlor without a blink. So did every other business owner on the strip.

Jossef was amazed that he didn't need an army. The newspaper and television stations were spreading the word about the Russian mob, starting with the bust in Miami and working out in all directions. They estimated that Samson, before his arrest by the DEA, had six hundred soldiers in South Florida, which Jossef figured was about right.

The media reported daily that the Russian mob was richer and more sophisticated than the Italian Mafia had ever been. They titillated their audience nightly with pictures and stories of atrocities committed by the Russians. Jossef even saw a picture of Big Tony, lying in a pool of blood on the sidewalk in front of his store, but the media had got it backward, announcing that Tony was an Italian, gunned down by the Russians.

The bartender from First Avenue who had witnessed the crooked-cop shooting, and had ten thousand new dollars at home in his pillowcase, estimated that there were twenty or more men who burst in waving rifles. No one seemed inclined to question the new rule of the Russian mob, so Jossef imported four more friends from Brooklyn for his army, and settled down to become the Don of Alaska.

He rather liked the role of respected businessman, so he stayed in the background and let the photogenic Yuri do the collecting. He swapped his Polaris Building penthouse for a mansion on Chena Ridge. From there, he could look down from his porch onto the Tanana River below him and see it winding in silver threads out of the vast Tanana Valley. Across the river to his right, Mt. Denali poked out of the Alaska Range, but snow-covered Mt. Deborah, standing straight south at the headwaters of the Wood River, was more spectacular.

Fairbanks nestled in the Chena Valley to his left, giving him the pleasure of surveying his fiefdom in the proper perspective, and his four soldiers had nothing to do but hang out and drink vodka.

Jossef had never bothered to determine exactly what services were provided by his massage parlor. The sign out front didn't mention S&M or B&D, but it did say *Full Body* and *Complete Satisfaction*. The day-to-day operation of the massage parlor was beneath Jossef's dignity, so he promoted Carla to manager.

Carla was misnamed; she should have been Brunhilda. Carla looked as if she were born in leather, and she carried a small whip dangling from her belt. At five foot eleven and 180 pounds, Carla made the classic silhouette, but the muscles bulging around the bra she wore on top, and beneath the micro-mini skirt below, could have belonged to an Olympic weight lifter. Jossef was confident that the parlor was in competent hands.

Chapter 7

I woke up around noon with bright sunshine streaming through the open balcony doors. Maggie had sprawled over considerably more than her half of the bed, with one hand in my face and one ankle across my leg. Her turban had slipped down to cover her face, and her still-damp hair spread over most of the bed. I got up, showered, and dressed in my dirty clothes. I was quiet about it, but I suspected that nothing less than a bomb would awaken Maggie. I did wish she'd cover her breasts. The ever-so-slightly-flattened cones that jiggled when she breathed, and neat little pencil-eraser nipples, made it hard to concentrate.

What is it about breasts? They come in all shapes and sizes, and an old girlfriend once pointed out that half the people in the world have them, but they are always fascinating, and the lines are always beautiful. They seem to connect directly with some very masculine hormones. I left a ten-dollar bill on the nightstand (not a payment or a loan, just more sharing), made it out of the room without biting anything, and took the elevator down to the coffee shop.

I sat next to the window to watch the world go by and ordered ham and eggs over easy, three glasses of orange juice, and a cup of coffee. I offered the orange juice as an appeasing sacrifice to the hangover that was threatening, used the coffee to finish waking up, and took out my urge to bite something soft and pliant on the ham.

The Malamute was in the midday doldrums. Several tables were occupied; some of the customers were already slumping badly or still slumped from the night before. The jukebox was wailing, Roy Orbison, I think, but no one was dancing. Renaldo poured me a glass of orange juice and brought it to a table by the front window. The pedestrians outside on Fourth Avenue, milling between bars, could have been on a different planet from the business-oriented parade I had just watched on Fifth.

Renaldo was immaculate and expansive, as always. He was wearing a white shirt with the sleeves rolled up precisely three turns for a casual effect, and gray slacks that were probably featured in *Esquire* magazine. He was in his executive mode that always reminds me of a runaway steamroller.

"Hey, we just missed the excitement last night. Couple of guys rammed their car into a light post and apparently the gas tank exploded. Must have been quite a show."

"No kidding," I told him. The orange juice was okay, but it came from a can, not from an orange.

"Got any coffee?" I asked.

Renaldo turned around and gave a high sign to a waitress. She was leaning against the bar wearing jeans, a red blouse, and running shoes: waitresses at the Malamute dressed for dispensing booze fast, not for sex appeal. Renaldo pantomimed drinking coffee, being very careful to grasp a cup handle with his thumb and one finger, pinkie extended, so it couldn't be mistaken for a glass or a beer bottle. She nodded and rushed right over with two cups of mud. I wondered if the expression "Here's mud in your eye" came from Renaldo's coffee, but I sure wasn't sleepy anymore after I tasted it.

Renaldo saw me wince. "Hey, that's the way the Eskimos like it. This is coffee for real men." He demonstrated by taking a big sip himself, and wincing, pretty much as I had.

"So, what's your plan?" he asked.

He had me there. I was still trying to shake cobwebs out of my head, but he expected an answer, so I said; "How about a meeting of all the bar owners on the street?"

"What, you want to start World War Three?"

"No, I'm serious." The notion had just popped out because I had to say something, but once it was out, it seemed like a good idea. "We have a common problem. We need to present a united front. The first thing we need to know is who these racketeers are, and you keep forgetting to ask them. Maybe some of the other victims are a little brighter. What say we invite everyone here for a drink after closing time?"

Renaldo gave me an exaggerated shrug, indicating that I'd lost my mind and he was humoring me. "Be my guest. If you can get them to come, I'll try to find some decent whiskey somewhere, maybe even some Captain Morgan's rum in case you're still alive."

I left the coffee, walked out onto Fourth, made it down the block to D Street without being accosted, and took the one-block walk to Fifth Avenue and a different world. On Fifth, Nordstrom's and Penney's were slugging it out for the daytime crowd, not a drunk in sight. I flipped a mental coin, went into Nordstrom's and bought six sets of underwear, three shirts, three pairs of pants, and six pairs of socks. I always buy the socks in a package, always black so that I never have to worry about matching them. My socks disappear at the usual rate, but as long as I still have two, they are a pair.

The sundries counter yielded a toothbrush, toothpaste, and a package of disposable razors. One of the toothpaste boxes showed the paste coming out in stripes and I wondered how they did that, so I bought that one. At the luggage counter, I picked up a bag like a bowling-ball bag, but big enough to contain all my new goodies.

I lugged my bag back to Renaldo's bar, changed in his office, and left the stash there. I wasn't about to go back to the room and confront Maggie's breasts. I started visiting the bar owners where E Street crossed Fourth Avenue and worked back toward C. My luck was just a little better than Renaldo's prediction.

All of the owners were old-timers, tougher than hickory and mad as hell, but they had spent so many years trying to cut each other's throats that a meeting was hard for them to swallow. There was a lot of profanity, but I got the impression that most of them were coming. I bombed out completely at the corner of D Street. The owner was a young guy, about Renaldo's age, new on the block, and he seemed to be more afraid of me than he was of the racket.

His name was Schneider, and he was almost all tan—tan hair, tan eyes, tan necktie, tan suit, tan shoes—but his skin was typical springtime Alaskan: fish-belly white. A pinkish scalp was beginning to show where his hair was thinning, and he had that slender, made-for-suits frame that one associates with bank tellers. He was immovable. His bottom line was that they hadn't killed him yet and he was still in business, so he wasn't going to rock the boat.

I was a little discouraged when I crossed D and tromped down the stairs to the Side Street. Pauline was behind the bar, but she motioned a waitress to take over and came out to sit in a booth with me. She was wearing a jade-green jumper, sexy in a Roaring Twenties way, and the color contrast was startling. Pauline had a lion's mane of flaming red hair, a figure that no dress could have contained, even if she had wanted it to, and a whiskey voice one octave lower than mine. You never would have guessed that she was over seventy years old and had been right there at the Side Street since Fourth Avenue was a dirt road and her customers were coming and going from WW II.

This may not be a delicate way to put it, but Pauline had more balls than all of the men I had talked to so far put together.

"You betcha, honey, I'll be there at three o'clock sharp, and I'll be packin' iron." I went on down the street, considerably encouraged.

At 2:45, Renaldo and I carried the last customers out and leaned them up on the sidewalk against the front of the building. We scooted tables together to make a boardroom effect and Renaldo proudly produced a bottle of Wild Turkey, a bottle of Cutty Sark, and a bottle of Captain Morgan. He plunked down an ice bucket between the bottles, a pitcher of ice water, and some cold cans of Coke for any sissies in the crowd, which turned out to be me.

At the stroke of 3:00, Pauline stomped in. I didn't see any iron, but she could have hidden a couple of .45s in her bosom with no problem. She picked up a glass, wiped it on her skirt, clinked in ice, poured the glass full of Wild Turkey, and sat down at the head of the table.

Renaldo and I joined her, and I did pop a can of Coke and splash some Captain Morgan into it, but I sat at the end of the table where I could watch the door, and my right hand was free, gun in pocket. A few minutes later, the parade of codgers started, most of them marching in, daring anyone to interfere. They were a motley crew, dressed in overalls, dungarees, plaid shirts, and several of them needing shaves. Physically, they covered the gamut from Rohrbaugh's six-foot-five to Harry's five-foot-six, but they all had the same expression, jaws tight and spoiling for a fight. They helped themselves to ice and tipped the bottles, most of them going for the scotch straight over rocks.

I was starting to get nervous because I had called the meeting and really didn't have much to say, but Pauline took charge. She whacked her half-empty glass on the table like a judge with a gavel, and the meeting was in session.

"I hear that you lily-livered ninnies have been paying protection money. Is that right?" She glared around the room and got some tentative nods.

Pinky, who owned the Union Club, had a great thatch of shaggy gray hair and eyebrows to match, but he was clean shaven and did have a spanked-baby-pink complexion. He was medium height, comfortably upholstered, and was almost man enough to stand up to Pauline.

"Do you mean that you haven't?" he asked.

"Of course not. I keep a sawed off double-barreled shotgun behind the bar and when that little pipsqueak came around, I let him look up the barrels and he scrabbled right up the stairs backward. The only reason I'm here is that a couple of my customers are telling stories about gunplay by Wyatt Earp here," she gave me a disdainful nod, "and I figure the car that blew up in the street was no accident. Maybe things are going to get serious, and maybe you need me to bail you out."

I didn't notice anyone about to disagree with her. The door eased open and a shadow slipped in. I had my gun on him in one half a heart thump, but it was the new guy from the corner, Mr. Tan who was so afraid of boat rocking. I was up anyhow, so I grabbed a glass off the bar, chunked ice into it, and set it down for him at the last vacant chair. He looked around the room, expecting to be shot at any moment, although I had put the gun away out of sight in my jacket pocket. His entrance did surprise me, though, so I walked over and snapped the deadbolt on the door.

He rushed to sit down, as if maybe he'd make a smaller target that way, and poured a shaky stream of the Captain Morgan straight over his ice, without the Coke.

"Well, well, Schnickelfritz himself," Pauline bellowed.

"It's Schneider," the newcomer squeaked.

Renaldo, ever the peacemaker, rushed to shake Schneider's hand and introduce himself. Pinky followed, so Avram, Harry, Rohrbaugh, and Alvarez followed suit, like a reception line at a funeral. Pauline gave him a disdainful nod, pretty much like the one she had given me, and the meeting came back to order.

"My idea is to shoot whoever comes to collect. All of you wimps have shotguns, or at least you used to, and pretty soon they'll stop coming." Pauline sat back, her bosom did one more leap, and she looked around expectantly.

"My God," Schneider breathed, "don't you people read the papers? Don't you know who we're up against here?"

Well, that got my attention because that was the main thing I wanted to know, but I wasn't prepared for his next statement.

"We're dealing with the Russian Mafia."

"How do you know that?" I blurted.

"They blasted into Fairbanks, blew away half the police force, took over the town, and a few weeks later they show up here. Who do you think it is?" Schneider buried his nose in the rum.

I had to admit that he had a good point there. I looked around the table and it only heightened the impression of a funeral . . . maybe ours. Everyone looked expectantly at Pauline.

"What the hell difference does that make?" she asked. "Russkies die of lead poisoning, just the same as everyone else." Pauline added an ice cube to her empty glass and chugged in Wild Turkey to the rim.

"Yeah," Pinky half stood and leaned against the table. "Problem is there's too many of them, and they'll just keep coming. I want to hear what Wyatt Earp has to say about that car blowing up. I was just coming out my door, and I saw you toss a burning bottle into the car, so what's your story?" Pinky sat back down, and everyone looked at me, Renaldo with a serious scowl.

"Okay," I said, "so they tried to burn the place down, and I tossed their Molotov cocktail back to them, that's all. Like Pauline said, Russkies burn up, just like everyone else."

Schneider had gone seriously pale. He tried to pour more rum and got almost as much on the table as he did in his glass. "I've read about how these guys operated in Brooklyn. Anyone who didn't pay, or just looked at them cross-eyed, simply disappeared, and the next day it was Russians running the businesses."

Pauline snorted "Well, that's not going to happen here, because if any Russkies show up running one of your bars, I'll personally blow them away." She turned a quizzical glance on Schneider. "Just what nationality is Schneider, by the by?"

Schneider threw his hands up as if someone had just pulled a gun on him. "It's German, pure German, but my only German ancestor came here before WW I and the rest of my ancestors are Irish." He looked at Pauline to see if it was okay to put his hands down, but she had turned to Pinky, so Schneider took a chance and grabbed a drink of his rum, spilling some more, which I really hated to see. If he was going to get so nervous and waste liquor, I wished that he'd switch to the bourbon; Pauline still had half a bottle left.

Pauline was addressing Pinky. "Weren't you some kind of a commando or something, back in the days when you still had balls?"

"Oh yeah, I was Special Forces, but that was thirty years ago. It was a little different situation."

"May not be so different, after all." We all turned to look at Avram, and he raised his glass to toast us. There was something classy about Avram, more like a schoolteacher than the lumberjacks the others brought to mind. His Silver Dollar Bar was as raunchy as the others, but he had a presence that made people listen when he spoke. Partly, it was his eyes, piercing, steady, but broadcasting calm. "I landed on Iwo Jima myself. Alvarez, didn't you hit the beach at Normandy?"

"Well, sure . . ." Alvarez, who was on the swarthy side and walked with a slight limp, cleared his throat and tried again, "sure I did, but I was carrying a bazooka, and it was pretty different. Besides, I got half my ass shot off, and I don't want to lose the other half."

"Well, I'll be damned," Pauline leaned back, shaking her lion's mane. "I've always said you were a half-assed bar owner but I never knew it was true."

A kind of a nervous titter spread around the table, and we didn't look so much like a funeral gathering anymore.

Renaldo's six-inch mustache was twitching, and I realized that was probably the longest he'd ever kept quiet in his life. He stood up, leaning forward, knuckles on the table.

"Okay, guys," he stopped and bowed to Pauline, "and madam, I think we're deciding to fight. We're our own little clique here, but together we represent less than ten percent of the bars in Anchorage. I nominate gun-happy Wyatt Earp to canvas the rest of them, see what he can learn, maybe get some consensus and report back to this committee in two days. What I'd like to know is where that Ed Asner guy hangs out when he's not holding us up. Has anyone ever seen him before?"

That brought a general round of negative grunts and Pauline stood up, so the meeting seemed to be over. Pauline made it official by draining her bourbon and smacking the glass of ice cubes down on the table. I unlatched the door and took a look outside. The area looked empty, but I kept my hand on my gun and walked out to the center of the street where I could see into the doorways. It looked safe, and people were streaming out and leaving anyway.

I watched until Pauline climbed into a block-long Cadillac sedan that was parked on D and burned rubber all the way around the corner onto Fourth and halfway to C Street. I went back into the bar and mixed a healthier rum and Coke.

Renaldo had put on his driving coat and gloves. "What say we hit the coffee shop at the Sheffield and get some breakfast?" he asked.

"No thanks, I think I'd better stick right here, just in case. We've got a good thing going, but I'd feel lousy if any of the bars got busted up tonight. You go to the Sheffield coffee shop, and here's a special assignment to help you earn your Boy Scout badge." I handed him my room key.

"You'll find a young lady waiting in the coffee shop. She's Yupik Eskimo, but I guess you wouldn't know the difference between that and Chinese. Anyway, she can sit on her hair and you can find her by following the alcohol fumes to their source. She answers to the name of Maggie. Just give her this key, and get out of her way so you don't get trampled."

Renaldo looked quizzical, but took the key and started out the front door.

"Hu-uh," I stopped him, "this way." I went to the back door and opened it. The alley was deserted, except for Renaldo's Alfa. He gave me a shrug, climbed in and pulled away down the alley. I closed and bolted the back door, then wandered up to the front windows to wonder what had possessed me to volunteer.

It was a long but quiet two hours. I dragged Renaldo's swivel chair out of his office and plunked down in it next to the window. I nursed the Captain Morgan along, but not enough to dull my senses. Every time I woke up, I checked the street and sat back down. The sun was up, the world looked pretty safe, and I had put the swivel chair back in the office when the first bartender arrived to open up at six in the morning. He was putting his key in the lock, and almost fainted when I pulled the door open. I gave him a friendly wave and headed for the coffee shop.

I wolfed down steak, eggs, and toast, along with a glass of milk, then stopped by the desk to tell them I'd lost my key. They gave me another, for two dollars and fifty cents added to my bill, and I leaned against the wall in the elevator, almost going to sleep on the way up to the eleventh floor.

Maggie was pretty well gathered on her own side of the bed, and snoring softly. With her mouth hanging open and her eyes closed, she looked like a little girl, sleeping on a black fan of hair. I heightened the little girl effect by very gently pulling the comforter up to cover her breasts, went around to my own side of the bed, and passed out in a reasonable length of time.

Chapter 8

Jossef paced his back porch, oblivious to the sunshine through the birch leaves that made mosaics on the redwood planks and to the half-mile-wide Tanana River racing by below him. He was furious, but he was also perplexed. In the old days, he would have shot Yuri's ears off for coming home with only fifteen thousand dollars instead of the hundred thousand he was supposed to bring and looking like he'd been worked over with a baseball bat.

When Jossef had got over the initial shock of Yuri's ignominious return from Anchorage, he had to admit that Yuri had been right not to continue his rounds. Yuri, looking like an underdone hamburger, would have given the wrong impression, and might have given someone else ideas. Jossef's fiefdom depended on the image of invincible Russians.

Jossef didn't know about the crazy broad at the Side Street Bar in Anchorage, or he would have shot Yuri's ears off. Yuri, figuring he'd lose some body parts either way, hadn't mentioned his encounter with the shotgun. He would have preferred not to mention the pool cue, but the cuts, creases, and lumps on his head made that encounter obvious.

Jossef's remaining Russian army had consisted of four soldiers: two Boris Karloffs and a Mutt and Jeff team. Jossef had sent the Karloffs to Anchorage to take over where Yuri left off, and they didn't come back. When he read about the car accident in Anchorage, with a picture of the burning car splashed across the front page of his *Daily News-Miner*, he jumped to the conclusion that the Italians must have organized Anchorage.

Jossef paused to lean his elbows on the railing and watch a jet, tiny in the distance, land at the Fairbanks airport, five miles away and a thousand feet below him but sharply defined in the crisp clear air. The jet turned off the runway, bringing more customers and more money to Fairbanks, and Jossef resumed his pacing.

He knew that his coup in Fairbanks, bloodless—unless you counted the crooked cops, which Jossef didn't—had been possible because neither the Italians nor the Russians had got there yet. Being up against the Italians in Anchorage would not have been a problem in the old days because Italians can't swim, particularly not with concrete blocks chained to their ankles and lead pellets in them here and there, but that was with a few hundred soldiers backing him up.

Jossef knew it had to be the Italians because he had attended a lecture by the Fairbanks police chief at a Chamber of Commerce meeting. The chief, resplendent in blue uniform, bristling with leather, guns, and badges, had advised the Americans at the chamber meeting on the proper way to deal with criminals. His message was to get out of the way and give them whatever they wanted.

"If you come home at night and find that your house has been broken into, don't go in because the burglar might still be there. Go to a neighbor's house and call the police." He then advised the neighbors that if anyone knocked on their door in the night, they shouldn't open the door, but it was okay to dial 911.

The six-foot-two, two-hundred-pound cop paced and gestured to make his points. "If you wake up at night and find someone burglarizing your house, pretend to stay asleep until they finish, and they might leave. If a thug demands your wallet on the street, give it to him, and hope he doesn't shoot you anyway."

All of that advice was strange to Jossef, but it was very good news. He thought it might make sense in America where money was easy to come by, even for the poor slobs who worked for it. In the old country, where people struggled, fought, and sometimes killed to get their money, they worked equally hard to keep it. That's why there was so little petty crime in the old country. If you demanded someone's money, one of you was going to die, and it wasn't always the intended victim.

Jossef looked at his last two soldiers, Boris and Ivan, sitting in folding chairs on the lawn beyond the porch, and the useless Yuri, who was lying on a reclining lawn chair trying to erase his headache with vodka. Jossef knew that the way to deal with Italians was to have twice as many soldiers as they had, and he decided he'd better do some recruiting. He hated to do that because keeping an army was expensive, and they rarely earned their keep. If a soldier did make money through some fluke, he usually stole it himself, anyway. It was because he wasn't supporting soldiers that Jossef was able to bring 98% of his earnings to the bottom line.

As a lad in Odessa, Jossef had been taught by his father that there are two ways of doing business. You can either skim the cream or kill the cow and eat the beef, but you can't do both. In Alaska, Jossef had been content to skim, partly because he didn't have a ready supply of immigrants to take over the businesses. He was secretly proud of the careful way in which he husbanded his flock. With extreme self-control, he had limited his skimming to those businesses that could produce $5,000 per month in cream and still survive. Further, he hadn't been greedy.

He had been content with just twenty businesses in Fairbanks and twenty in Anchorage, just $200,000 per month, bringing a bit over two million per year to the bottom line. (He didn't know, of course, that Yuri's rounds in Anchorage were actually twenty-three clubs, one to make up for the crazy broad in the Side Street with the shotgun, and two for Yuri's personal retirement fund.) Yes, skimming the cream had been good, but he decided it was time to do a little butchering.

He stopped pacing his porch and looked down the bluff at the river where Captain Binkley's sternwheeler was going by with a load of happy tourists. Jossef thought it wasn't right for the tourists to be singing and laughing when he himself had problems, and he was tempted to machine-gun the lot of them. That would have felt good, but he knew it wasn't smart business. He stomped inside to his office to make some phone calls.

He dialed Big Tony's grocery store in Brooklyn. Big Tony was gone to his reward, thank heaven, but the store would still be the headquarters, and whoever had taken over would not blame Jossef for doing his husbandly duty. The phone burred twice and was picked up with, "Whatcha want?" Jossef asked for the manager, and the phone was dropped on a counter. When the manager came on, he didn't sound right. Jossef had expected to recognize the voice and had wondered which lieutenant had taken over.

"Who's this?" Jossef asked.

"This is Angelo Titalia, the owner. What the hell do you want?"

Jossef hung up the phone and hoped that he might have dialed a wrong number. He picked up again and dialed the flower shop back on his own beat on Avenue Z.

"Feinberg's Flower Shop." Feinberg had given up the grocery business and moved down the street to become a florist after the unfortunate drug buy in his grocery store.

"Hey, Feinberg, how's it hanging?"

"Straight up and pointing. Who is this?"

That struck Jossef as strange. Feinberg should have recognized his voice— it had only been a few years—and if he didn't, he shouldn't have asked on the telephone anyway. Jossef switched to Russian and asked how the business was doing. Feinberg switched too, but not to the rich, colorful mother tongue of Odessa. The phony Feinberg was speaking the childish diplomatic Russian that the American feds used. Jossef slammed down the receiver.

He realized he had just been tape-recorded by the DEA and his call was being traced, probably not to Chena Ridge, but at least to Fairbanks, Alaska. Jossef knew all about the DEA tape recording, because they had produced hundreds of hours of taped phone calls at Samson's trial. The juicier recordings had been leaked to the national magazines. Jossef would have been impressed when he read that Samson was brokering a thirty-million-dollar deal to sell a Russian attack submarine to a South American tour company, if Samson hadn't already been in a federal lockup.

Jossef stomped out of the office, through the living room, and into the big sunny kitchen. He pulled a glass from the freezer, held it under the ice dispenser for two counts and splashed in what he thought of as "that Stolichnaya piss" sold as vodka in Fairbanks. He took a sip, wrinkled his nose, and continued out to the yard where his army sat playing checkers at a lawn table in the shade of a cottonwood tree. They seemed to be evenly matched. They had made all the free moves, so someone was going to be jumped. Both stared at the board and apparently no one was planning to move.

Ivan was good solid Russian stock, five-foot-nine and two hundred pounds. He had a square head mounted on massive shoulders with no visible neck, and the same animated expression as the tree. Boris had been six-foot-six, but after years of stooping down to go through doorways, he had stopped straightening up. He weighed probably less than a 150 pounds, but he was an asset. His gray, dissipated, cadaverous physiognomy radiated evil. Yuri was stretched out on his lawn chair, moaning in his sleep, with an empty bottle on the grass beside him.

Jossef's immediate problem was that there were sixteen more bars in Anchorage waiting to contribute their $5,000 for the month, and he hated to disappoint them. He looked at Ivan and Boris, said, "eeny meeny miney moe," and decided to send both of them, but maybe telling them to skip the Malamute Saloon, which was apparently the Italians' headquarters.

Chapter 9

I t was Renaldo's idea that I should use the Alfa Romeo, and it was not the first time that one of his ideas had nearly killed me.

"Go easy," he said. "It's got the V-6 in it, almost 3,000 cc, so don't be stomping on the gas."

As if I'd never driven a car before. I started it up in the alley: "rrr, rrr, vroom." Just like my pickup truck, only a little more vroom. I read the diagram on the shift knob, put it in first, and eased out the clutch. Tires screamed and my head snapped back against the headrest. If I hadn't been wearing a seat belt, I might have ended up behind the seat, along with my hat.

Naturally, my reaction was to step on the brake, which slammed my forehead against the steering wheel. I tried again, using second gear and letting the engine idle, and made it to the end of the alley. I turned the wheel in the normal manner for a right turn, and pretty nearly went down the sidewalk instead of the street. I missed the parking meter, bounced off the curb, made it down E Street to Fourth Avenue, and ever so gently braked for the stoplight. I was on my way.

It was a little like a Saturday night in my twenties, hitting every bar in the city, only this time I wasn't having a drink in every one. I was having solemn, or sometimes hysterical, conversations with the owners or managers.

I had started just after noon when Maggie rolled over and slapped me in the chops with her still-sleeping hand, and I was still going at 3 AM when bars started closing. I had learned a few things. The big hotels that had security cameras, armed guards on duty, and direct lines to the police had not been bothered. Neither had the small operations that were just squeaking by.

I was getting the impression of a route. The appropriate bars had all been hit on Fourth Avenue down as far as Gambell. Then, the collector apparently turned right on Gambell, hit the bars and the Finlandia

Steam Bath, and followed Gambell to Fireweed Lane. He turned right again, followed Fireweed to Spenard Road, then left on Northern Lights Boulevard, and back to Gambell, which by that time had become the Seward Highway.

I had counted eighteen bars on the route. Most of the proprietors had figured the Russian connection, were grateful and a little surprised to be still alive, and I heard several more lectures about rocking boats. The most surprising thing I learned, or seemed to have learned, was that all of the collections were made on about the same day, or within two days.

I parked the Alfa in the alley and took the keys in to Renaldo. He was in his counting house, counting out his money. He gave me a quizzical glance, I gave him a "so-so" hand wobble, he went back to his counting, and I walked back to the Sheffield House.

It seemed that the Ed Asner guy just appeared, worked fast, and disappeared again. I wished to heck I knew where to, and I was still pondering that when I pulled the comforter up to Maggie's chin and passed out. . . . Okay, so I did have a drink in each of the last four bars I had visited.

I woke up when the sun blasted in through the French doors, which made it almost noon. Maggie was gone, but she had left one clean towel in the bathroom, so I took a good long hot shower. That might seem like a strange thing to report, but if you live in Bethel where chocolate-brown water is delivered by city trucks and costs six cents a gallon, then a long, hot shower deserves reporting.

I walked back to the Malamute and picked up the Alfa with considerably more confidence. It did seem strange, though, looking up at all the other cars, including the Volkswagen Beetles, and watching the traffic ahead by looking under the trucks. I stopped for a mid-afternoon breakfast at one of the W Plazas that were spread around the edges of the city.

The "W" stood for Pete Weinberger. Legend had it that Pete was a marked man, under a *hit* sentence by some mob back East. He had moved to Anchorage but he wasn't hiding out. He owned the biggest mansion in the classy Turnagain Arm area, complete with a forty-foot-tall pillared porte-cochère that would have done a Greek temple proud. The evidence that supported the legend was that he had painted his mansion bright purple, so that if anyone dared to look for him, he'd be easy to find. I don't know the truth of the legend, but the purple mansion is true, and once you've seen it, you're not likely to forget it.

Anyhow, I blessed Pete for having twenty-four-hour breakfasts available and got back to my bar canvassing. I headed out of town, following the route on Seward Highway, and ran out of pay dirt. I turned back to Dimond Boulevard and was back on the track. Dimond is the right spelling, by the way. The boulevard was named for Judge Dimond, not for the gem. I had counted either twenty-two or twenty-three bars, depending on whether you counted Pauline's Side Street, and that was the end of it. Asner just stopped, and at a strange number. I figured his monthly take at $110,000.

I tried all the side roads and continued all the way down Dimond to Minnesota Drive. That led me back to International Airport Road, but no more customers. It struck me that if you ignored a few detours, I had traced a half-circle that started at a logical place on Fourth Avenue and ended at the airport. I wondered if that accounted for Asner's never being seen between collections, and if he came by airplane, just where had that flight originated? Russia seemed unlikely.

At a quarter to three in the morning, Renaldo and I set up the boardroom. Renaldo had brought two bottles of Cutty Sark, another Wild Turkey, and another Captain Morgan. Pauline stomped in promptly at three, overloaded her glass with Wild Turkey, and plunked down at the head of the table. I stood by the door, pistol in hand, and checked the arrivals.

The Fourth Avenue cadre was intact. All of my proselytizing had produced only four warm bodies from the off-Fourth bars. They were younger, cleaner, and looked more like bar owners, but they didn't sit at the directors' table. They carried their drinks to adjacent tables and settled in to kibitz, or maybe just watch us hang ourselves.

Pauline brought us to order with a whack of her glass on the table, glared at me and said, "Well?"

I stood up, cleared my throat. Nothing came out, so I cleared my throat again, and tried to think. Forget that. I just told them what I had found out and the apparent route leading toward the airport. That was met with stony silence and the expectant stares continued, so I tried again.

"Look," I said, "when this guy picks up the vigorish, does he ever count it?"

That brought a general round of chin and head scratching, some conferring, and a general consensus that he didn't; he just took the bags, each of which was supposed to contain $5,000. It struck me that six-foot-five Rohrbaugh from the Four Aces, who could have been a one-man football line, spoke in the quiet gentle voice of a Sunday school teacher, while five-foot-six Harry from the Paradise Club had a basso profundo reminiscent of James Earl Jones.

"Okay," I tried again. "The collections got interrupted, but they'll be back for the rest. We need to know a lot more about these guys, and maybe the easiest way is to follow them and see where they go."

That brought some headshakes and negative grunts, but I plunged ahead. "I'll do the following, and this time they'll be looking for trouble, so you should just hand over the cash . . . only anyone who has the guts might as well cut up some dollar-bill-sized newspaper strips and band a couple of hundreds to the outside to make bundles. They'll be pissed, but if it's all in paper bags, they won't know who stiffed them. Maybe by next month, if we learn enough and figure a way, they won't be back."

I saw the squinty gleam in Pinky's eyes, and Alvarez was calmly nodding his head. Alvarez was the only one of the scotch drinkers who added water, and the only one who still had some black hairs sprinkled through the gray. I'm not saying that's cause and effect; more likely the black was South American genes. I think Schneider was just going to pay off, and so were the spectators from the country club set, but I felt better about suggesting that they pay if they had an option.

I took a deep breath and turned to the head of the table. "Pauline, we need your cooperation here. Things are escalating. First they sent one bagman and you were right to chase him away. Next they sent two heavies packing cannons, but they never made it to the Side Street. The next wave may be very big and very bad. I don't mean that you couldn't handle the situation, but for the sake of the rest of us, I'm asking you to at least pretend to pay them. If you'll do that, I can follow them, but if you blow them away, we'll have to wait for bigger and bigger armies."

Pauline gave me a disdainful sniff, clearly indicating that I was selling out to the enemy.

"All right, Wyatt, we'll try it your way once, but if it doesn't work, kablowie."

I wasn't sure if the "kablowie" was for me or for the next wave of Russians. This time I had been thinking, and this time I did have a plan. "Renaldo, what's the number of your private line in your office?" Renaldo spit it out; most of the attendees wrote it down. "Tomorrow, all you have to do is dial that number after the collectors have visited. Any questions?" I got the impression that they would all make the call, even the spectators, and we adjourned on a reasonably upbeat note. Pauline stood up, drained her glass, whacked it on the table, and we all trooped out.

Renaldo and I hit the Sheffield coffee shop, took a booth by the window, and ordered strawberry waffles and coffee.

"Well, Einstein, just what is this brilliant plan of yours?" Renaldo approached his coffee warily, took a sip, and relaxed when he realized it was potable.

"Well, it's going to tie you up in the office, answering the phone for a few hours. I'll bring you a walkie-talkie for communicating with me. Think you can handle that?"

"Can do." Renaldo was nodding, the tips of his mustache just out of sync. "Then what?"

"Then I follow them."

The waitress brought our waffles and was standing in front of the table when Maggie stumbled through the door. Maggie plunked down at the counter, waved my room key, and ordered steak and eggs. She didn't look around. She was twenty feet away with her back to us, concentrating on trying not to spill her coffee.

"You know, that car of mine is a little obvious. You'll be easy to spot." I'm not sure if Renaldo's concern was for me or the Alfa.

"Don't worry about it," I told him. "I'm going to be so inconspicuous that my mother couldn't find me in a cradle."

We concentrated on our waffles, laden with real strawberries, sliced and smothered in fake whipped cream. Maggie was served and wolfed down her steak like a vacuum cleaner. The waitress came to refill our coffee. Maggie finished eating, signed the tab charging her breakfast to my room, and marched off toward the lobby. I dawdled over the coffee. Renaldo gave up and went home, leaving me the tab. I had one more cup, went over the possibility that my plan might work, and drank so slowly that the coffee got cold before I figured Maggie would be asleep and it was safe to go up to the room. The toothpaste did come out of the tube in stripes, but I still don't know how they do that.

By the middle of the next afternoon, I had conned Joe Wilbur into renting me his Brantly helicopter. He may have said something, maybe he just looked at me, but I got the idea that I was overstaying my transient welcome. I taxied the 310 up to the pumps and we topped off the tanks, seventy-six gallons of hundred octane. I moved it to a regular tie-down, which Joe was happy to rent to me for $20 per day. Then I rented one of Joe's handheld aircraft-band radios for another ten dollars a day. Joe keeps a few of those, batteries always charged, because Anchorage is a terminal control zone. You may not operate within it without a radio. If your radio fails and you want to wait until you get back to Bethel or wherever to fix it, you rent one of Joe's radios to get out of the control zone. A few Piper J-3 cubs are still operating around Anchorage, maybe even a Taylorcraft or two, that have no radios, and in fact, no electrical systems. If you want to fly one of those around Anchorage, your solution is to make Joe a little richer.

The Brantly looks like a toy. It might be the smallest helicopter ever made, and I half suspect it's a Disney design. It has a bubble barely big enough for two small people to squeeze into, the outline of an ice cream cone sideways, and a three-bladed rotor that droops down almost to the ground when it isn't turning, but the Brantly is as real as helicopters get. The ratio of power to weight is twice as good as the Bell 47 that everyone recognizes from M*A*S*H. That short, flexible, three-bladed rotor makes the Brantly unbelievably maneuverable. If I get stuck with the job of setting someone on a mountain, say in Turnagain Pass where the wind always howls sixty or more, and the updrafts would tear a glider apart, I want to be flying the Brantly.

I went back to Renaldo's bar and perched in his office to phone every owner or manager and be sure they all had Renaldo's private number. Then I left Renaldo puzzling over the aircraft radio. "Just push this button to talk. Notice that the frequency is set to 122.8. That's Wilbur's Unicom frequency so don't change it. He'll be closed for the night, so that's your private line to me, kapish?" Renaldo nodded, and pushed the button a few times to practice. The radio said, "Aircraft calling Wilbur's Unicom, we are receiving your carrier, but no modulation. Please check your microphone." Renaldo put the radio down on his desk.

A tiny coffee shop with six stools is squeezed in next to the entrance to the Silver Dollar. I ignored the racket, got a good hamburger, excellent fries, and drinkable coffee. I grabbed a cab back to Merrill Field.

At midnight, I was sprawled across the seat in the Brantly, feet jammed against the bubble on the left, back resting against the right side, head jammed against the bubble on top. Blue lights from the taxiway beside me gave the illusion of moonlight, but it was actually a very dark night. White lights along the two runways merged into illustrations of perspective drawings, and the lighted cab on top of the tower on the other side of the runways was the only indication of life.

I had a pound of mixed nuts, a six-pack of Cokes, and a copy of Dostoevsky's *The Idiot*. I used a penlight to read by, and the reflection of light off the bubble doubled its brightness. I can recommend that book for any long vigil. You can read it for hours, have no idea what, if anything, is going on, pick it up anywhere and keep reading, but for some reason you never get sleepy.

I had the master switch and the radio on, radio tuned to 122.8. Renaldo's call woke me at 2:30.

"Hello, are you there?"

"One if by land, two if by sea, are the British coming?" I knew that wasn't right, but there was a giant cobweb stuck in my brain.

"I doubt it's the British, but whoever. Schneider just called. Two guys came in with guns in their hands, grabbed the sack and went out in tandem, the tall thin one covering the door and the bar, the short stocky one walking backward and keeping his gun on Schneider. They climbed into a big white sedan and drove it across the street to Pauline's."

"Roger. Listen for shotgun blasts. I'll call you back in five minutes."

I put the book down, not bothering to mark my place, and stomped on the heel-pedal to crank the Brantly. The engine roared. Because it's so short, the blade spun up fast, the needles locked, engine and blade made all one piece by the centrifugal clutch. I put the headset for the radio on my left ear. I wound the engine up to 2400 rpm, which put the blade at 900, and switched the radio to tower frequency. The controller and I were the only two people at the airport, so my clearance was instant. In a chopper, the throttle is part of the collective lever, like the throttle on a motorcycle. I cranked in power, sucked up the collective to increase the pitch on the blades, and the Brantly leapt into the air as if gravity had been repealed.

I climbed straight up to five hundred feet so it would be legal to fly over people, scooted toward Fourth Avenue while I climbed to a thousand feet, and then committed the two ultimate no-nos. I turned off the clearance lights. That would be a bad thing if another airplane came along, but it did make me inconspicuous. I switched the radio back to Unicom frequency, which would probably get me the electric chair if Anchorage Radio noticed I was still in the control zone and not talking to them.

"Did you go to sleep at your post yet?"

"Haven't had time. Pauline just called, and I quote: 'Okay, Junior, I let those two punks out of here alive. You owe me two hundred bucks.' She slammed down the receiver."

"Okay, we're off and running. A white sedan is coming toward me on Fourth. It's perfect for following. I think he's going to pull into the lot at the Fireside Lounge. Keep me posted."

Traffic was thinning out for the night. I made two circles at the corner of Fourth Avenue and Gambell. The sedan stopped at the Fireside Lounge. Five minutes later, the sedan pulled out of the lot and Renaldo was on the horn.

"Eric just called, blubbering that he handed over the sack, but they shot his pet goldfish anyhow, and there was water all over his desk."

"Gotcha. The sedan is headed down Gambell. Hold my calls for the next ten minutes."

"You stopping for coffee?"

"No, I'm going to try to keep my pilot's license for a while." I called Anchorage Center, told them I was on a photographic assignment, planning to circle downtown below one thousand feet for the next hour. I did not tell them my lights were off, and they gave me their blessing. That was crucial because they had been watching me on radar since I took off. I hoped they assumed I was still talking to Merrill Tower; anyhow, they hadn't called in any National Guard fighter planes yet.

Flying a helicopter at night is a special experience. It's all done with instruments because a chopper is too sensitive to fly by feel without a solid horizon. The instruments are clustered nicely on a pedestal by your right knee, and you're using all of them. In an airplane, you just trim it and forget it. In a helicopter, raising the collective a quarter inch will have your rpm dropping off and the chopper going up like a balloon. You just lock onto the soft red glow of the instruments and stay there, but following the car, kind of with peripheral vision, was not a problem.

People always ask which is easier to fly, airplanes or helicopters. I tell them that the two are so different that you can't compare them. In an airplane, you stay alive by keeping your speed up. In a helicopter, you don't care about airspeed; you can be backing up, but you stay alive by keeping your rotor speed in the tiny green tick on the RPM arc, and you stay in the right part of the sky by watching your manifold pressure.

We left Fourth Avenue, worked our way down Gambell, and the car stopped at the Finlandia Massage Parlor for fifteen minutes while I made circles in the air. That was not a good place to be, because we were pretty close to the approach to the north-south runway at Merrill Field. Luckily no jets showed up. Eventually, we worked on down the hill on Gambell and climbed up to the lesser-populated Fireweed Lane. I switched the radio back to Unicom.

"Still with me?"

"Welcome back. Vera called from the Finlandia to report that a couple of nice new guys showed up, collected her money, and had a cup of tea. She opined that I sounded tense and should probably come in for a massage. She has four new girls just arrived from the Philippines. Which assignment do you figure is more important?"

"For $5,000 per month? You wrestle with that problem. I'll call you back." I switched the radio back to Anchorage Center. Still no fighter jets on the way.

The clock on the pedestal said 3:45 when we got to the intersection of Fireweed and Spenard. We worked the two blocks farther from town on Spenard Road, but instead of turning down Northern Lights Boulevard, the car headed out of town, jogged left on International to the corner of Arctic Boulevard, and pulled into the parking lot at the Thunderbird Motel. It parked in a back corner of the lot and two guys, one tall, one wide, wandered into the motel carrying overnight bags.

I switched back to Unicom and called Renaldo. He sounded a little tense.

"Where the hell have you been?"

"Since you were busy, I stopped by Finlandia for you. Pick me up at Wilbur's flight service on Merrill Field, right across from the coffee shop, and step on it."

I tilted the Brantly toward home, turned on the lights and cranked in the power, switched the radio to tower frequency and woke up the operator. I had just tied down the blade when Renaldo came screeching off Fifth Avenue.

Chapter 10

The parking lot at the Thunderbird Motel was pretty dark, but I would have preferred darker. Renaldo parked the Alfa in the first available slot, next to the street, and we walked between rows of cars back toward the spot where the bagmen had parked. The big white car gleamed dully at the end of the line, looking like a ghost in the semi-darkness. It turned out to be a Chrysler. I dug a business card that I didn't recognize anymore out of my wallet and wrote down the license number, then walked around back and found the Avis sticker in the rear window.

I thought how great it would be to get a look at the contract and tried the doors, but the car was locked. Suddenly I heard a window scrape open on the second floor, thirty yards away. I grabbed Renaldo's sleeve and hit the pavement behind the car just as a volley of automatic fire chewed up the lot behind us. Things had been pretty quiet, so the burst of gunfire sounded awfully loud, and sort of obscene. We bounded toward the street, running fast behind the cars on all fours like a couple of bears.

The line of cars wasn't solid enough. Bullets stayed right with us, bouncing off cars, breaking windshields, chewing up pavement. I stopped and backed up past a couple of cars. I could see the muzzle flashes coming from a window, so I put two .38 slugs in the same spot and the shooting stopped. We made it past four more cars, and I was thinking we could stand up and run for it when the shooting started again.

We hunkered down behind the last car in the line, a big Buick that was backed into the space, and the Buick's windows exploded. We were shaking glass fragments out of our hair and off our shoulders when the bullets hit the gas tank. The explosion sounded like Krakatoa. The car jumped forward three feet and knocked us sprawling. We'd have been sitting ducks on the pavement, but a fountain of flames shot up, and the next second the gas tank on the car behind the Buick exploded. With a wall of fire between us and the motel, we ran for the street, jumped over the three-foot rock wall, and kissed the sidewalk.

It was hard to believe that the apparition facing me with an accusing stare was Renaldo. He was sort of sparkling in the streetlights with glass fragments all over his clothes and in his hair. His eyebrows and the tips of his mustache were singed and drooping, and he smelled like a wet dog. He was giving me the same sort of disapproving perusal.

Sirens came screaming down International from the direction of the airport, and a moment later, more sirens were coming up Arctic Boulevard. We crawled to the end of the fence, around the corner out of sight under some weeds, and just hugged the ground. Cops and fire trucks came from everywhere; floodlights made the parking lot daytime and put us in a deep shadow. We stayed put.

In half an hour, the fire trucks began to leave, then a few police cruisers slipped away. The floodlights were gone, so it was okay to sit up and look over the fence. There was only one cop car left, parked at the entrance to the office, and the big white Chrysler was no longer parked in its spot. We stood up, still shaking off glass, and strolled like innocent bystanders past the lot. When we got to the Alfa, we stepped over the fence. Renaldo waved me away, dug a blanket out from behind the seat, and covered the leather with it before he let me get in.

Maggie was lying on her side, snoring softly. Maybe *snore* isn't the right word; that has a disagreeable masculine connotation to it. What Maggie was doing was more of a purr, very soft and very feminine, with just enough movement to vibrate her breasts and set her nipples to dancing.

She had used only three towels, so there were three clean ones left, and I used two of them before I stopped raining glass. That was tricky because I sure didn't want to rub in the glass, so I tried to rinse it off, then used a little bottle of shampoo that the hotel had provided. I patted it all over my body and rinsed again. When I tried a tentative rub across my hair, it didn't feel gritty anymore.

I woke up early when someone dropped a tray full of dishes in the hall. Maggie hadn't moved, unless you count the vibration and the nipple dancing. I had breakfast in the coffee shop downstairs and wandered down Fifth Avenue to E Street, then cut over to Fourth and noticed that the Alfa wasn't parked in the alley. I actually ordered, and tried to drink, another cup of Renaldo's coffee before he came in.

Renaldo had done a pretty good job of art restoring, except his eyebrows were thinner than usual and he had snipped an inch off each end of his mustache. Some nasty red burn marks on his cheeks and forehead contrasted with his tan. He tossed me the keys to the Alfa when he went by and kept on stalking right into his office and closed the door. I understood that Renaldo would not want to be seen for a couple of days, until he had completely recovered. I was in just as bad shape, but no one, including me, has ever worried about how I look.

I drove out to the airport, actually found a parking spot in the garage, and took the escalator down to the arrivals area and the car rental booths. The girl running the Avis counter seemed to be having her first day on the job, and didn't know from nothing. You get that a lot in Alaska. I'd give odds that she was a military wife, her husband stationed at one of the bases. The husband would be on a two-year assignment, and sadly, the wives rarely last the whole term. She was a cute kid, perky little face and dark brown pageboy, but her big brown eyes got bigger and she seemed ready to panic when I started asking about the Chrysler.

I helped her panic along by flopping my badge out on the counter. It's a heavy silver affair, plenty of engraving, and it says "Detective" across the face in blue letters. It doesn't say "private" so if you don't know better, you might think there's something official about it. I'm careful never to say that, because impersonating an officer is a felony, but I sometimes don't burden people with unnecessary explanations.

"Look, Trisha," I read her name off the badge that was perched dangerously at the apex of her left breast, "we're on the same side here. As the official representative of Avis, it is your duty and privilege to help law enforcement in any way you can. Just enter the license number into your computer and see what comes up."

She pecked in the numbers, stared at the screen a while, then dug through a pile of contracts and pulled one out. She tentatively slid it across the desk toward me, a tentative smile matching her gesture. I gave her the full thousand-watt, official law-enforcement smile.

The car had been turned in at nine o'clock that morning. It had been rented by a Mr. O. J. Jones, a salesman with a Seattle address: 5517 East Madison Street. I'm not an expert on Seattle, but to Alaskans, a trip to Seattle is sort of the equivalent of a pilgrimage to Mecca, or maybe Jerusalem.

Most Alaskans have visited the University of Washington, if they didn't actually graduate from there, so we know that 55th Street is up around the

University District. We also know most of the city parks, so we know that East Madison Street angles east toward a park and the lake. It seemed to me that a 5500 block address on East Madison would be in the middle of Lake Washington. I dutifully copied the address anyhow, because Trisha expected me to, patted her hand when I slid the contract back, and went out to the Alfa.

At the Thunderbird Motel, the parking lot looked like a carnival in progress. Three television remote trucks were parked around the office door, with forty-foot masts swaying gently to support microwave antennas. Some of the cars that were parked crosswise of the drive were marked *Daily News* and *Anchorage Times*. A kelly-green Volkswagen was emblazoned *Penny Saver*. Various cars had call letters and slogans for radio stations and bristled with antennas of the twelve-inch variety. I parked the Alfa, took out my notebook and a pen, and eased into the crowd in the office.

The star of the show was in her sixties, but dressed and made up in a way that I doubted was her usual mode. She looked like Oprah may look in thirty years. There were six or eight microphones jammed in her face, and the television cameramen all had Sun Guns trained on her, so she needed to talk fast before she started to sweat.

I gleaned a sound bite for my personal newscast. Two men, a Mr. Jones and a Mr. Brown from Seattle, had rented a room. During the night, one of them went crazy and started shooting up the parking lot from his window. They had damaged or destroyed twenty-seven cars and burned up three cars completely. The perpetrators had escaped before the cops got there, but she herself had supplied the police with the men's Seattle addresses, so they would be apprehended shortly. The Thunderbird had absolutely no liability in the case. A brand new sign on the driveway announced that parking was at the car owner's risk.

I wandered back to the Alfa before the news crews started photographing the empty parking spots where the cars had been. The slot where the Buick had been parked was pretty well charred, and there was still plenty of glass around for the photographers, so it wasn't a total waste.

On careful analysis of the data I had collected so far, I reached several conclusions. Some were that the bagmen were not named Brown or Jones, and almost as certainly, they were not from Seattle. That last bit was poignant because it didn't leave many alternatives, and I started to wonder about Schneider's statement that the Russians had taken over Fairbanks. It was time to do some actual detecting.

Chapter 11

Jossef wasn't surprised when Ivan and Boris reported that they'd been ambushed and attacked by twenty-five or thirty Italians. Ivan had a new .38 caliber bullet in his shoulder that Jossef had to dig out with a pair of long-nosed pliers. Ivan's solid Russian frame had absorbed several bullets over the years, and he didn't much mind one more.

The bullet Jossef dug out was soft-nosed, so it had torn an ugly hole but stopped before it broke the bone. Jossef grabbed the bottle of vodka that Ivan was sucking on, and doused the wound with the alcohol. He handed the bottle back to Ivan, who went into his pacifier mode again, hardly noticing the interruption. He meandered out into the back yard to sit and stare at the checkerboard; Jossef went into his office to assess the situation.

He was shocked and saddened when he discovered that two of the $5,000 packets consisted of a couple of bills on the outside and neatly cut newspaper inside. It was getting so that you just couldn't trust anyone anymore. It seemed like business ethics were a thing of the past. One bundle seemed lumpy. He pulled the rubber band off, gave a shriek and dropped the bundle when a mousetrap snapped shut and a confetti of toilet paper fluttered to the floor. Things were definitely getting out of hand.

He figured that the number of Italian soldiers, estimated as twenty-five by Boris and thirty by Ivan, was an exaggeration. If it had been Jossef himself, reporting the same numbers to Big Tony, then the actual count of Italians was probably less than twenty. He figured that he had no choice, he had to recruit at least forty soldiers, and hang the expense. It wasn't so much that he was still short $30,000 from the Anchorage collection, it was that his authority as the Don of Alaska was being questioned, and Dons cannot afford that. They must retain their honor at any cost.

He thought about the two Dons from Seattle whom he had entertained in Miami. They should be very grateful to him. Not only had he provided exactly the entertainment they had requested, he had procured two of the women afterward and supplied the two Dons with their own whips, although the thongs were denim instead of leather. He hoped that they might lend him some soldiers, for old time's sake.

Jossef was apprehensive about leaving money lying around in his absence. Even though it was in a locked floor safe under the mat that was under his desk in his locked office, you just never knew. His army might decide to give the place a good cleaning while he was gone; heaven knows the place could use it. If they were cleaning and discovered his office door locked, they would consider it reasonable to shoot the lock off, and if they happened to be vacuuming under the mat that was under his desk, and the vacuum cleaner happened to twirl the knob and pop the safe open, then they would conclude that he had left them an early Christmas bonus.

He packed his carry-on bag full of cash, checking to see that all the bundles were from the good old days when his customers were still honest. But then he had to take $10,000 out to make room for a spare pair of beautiful red socks and the flowered boxer shorts that he might need in a couple of days. He packed the floor safe full of cash and stood on the lid to close and lock it, replaced the mat and the desk, and stuffed the last few hundred thousand in his jacket pockets.

Yuri was mooning around the empty refrigerator in the kitchen, so Jossef magnanimously handed him a hundred bucks to buy groceries, and recruited him to drive the Mercedes to the airport. In Anchorage, Jossef glanced around the terminal fearfully but didn't see any Italians. He caught an Alaska Airlines 727 and eventually found himself once again shivering outside the terminal at Seattle's Sea-Tac Airport.

He walked down the line of taxis that were waiting on the street, but none of the drivers looked Russian. He settled for a Filipino and was whisked down freeways, over viaducts, under viaducts, through viaducts, and finally veered off Highway 99 onto a roller coaster track between the pilings and straight down a toboggan chute, across railroad tracks and Alaska Way, to the Edgewater Hotel.

A sign in the lobby offered fishing poles for rent and he understood why when he opened the drapes in his room and found himself hanging out over Elliot Bay. A steady queue of container ships, tankers, yachts, sailboats, and ferries paraded past. He noticed a line of debris, organized by some current or tide, right outside his window. When he looked closer, he saw that half the flotsam was used condoms, so he knew he was getting close to his objective.

His problem was that Mafiesky Dons do not advertise in the Yellow Pages. He remembered the name Seidel, but there was no point looking in the phone book for that, either. He trudged across Alaska Way and up the hill, through the Pike Street Market with its piles of fresh fruit, vegetables, and fish, and down the city canyon of First Avenue until he saw a drug deal going down in a dirty stone doorway. Sure enough, the seller was Russian.

He passed his urgent request for a meeting with Seidel, and a hundred-dollar bill, to the seller and then spent two days hanging around his hotel and the waterfront, wondering why Seattleites don't all die of boredom, if not from the cold. He checked out the aquarium, which was nothing but a bunch of fish. There were numerous sex shops on First and Second Avenues, but they were the type where you put a quarter in a slot to watch some grandmother take off her clothes and wiggle her cellulite for two minutes.

On the morning of the third day, while he was perking the third pot of coffee from the single pad of grounds in his in-room Mr. Coffee, his phone rang and he was told to stand outside in the parking lot. Jossef stood just past the valet parking alley, looking up at the hill and the viaduct that offered a million places for a sniper to be hiding, but a limousine skidded to a stop and two heavies jumped out. Jossef was frisked, pretty damn personally he thought, and shoved into the back seat between the heavies.

The limousine screeched up the hill, through a tunnel, onto viaducts and freeways, then over miles of floating bridge across what looked like more ocean, to a sign that read Mercer Island. One of the heavies grabbed Jossef's arms, the other tied a blindfold onto him. When he was dragged out of the car and the blindfold removed, he was inside a courtyard with twelve-foot-high stone walls and enough trees to start a logging operation.

He was marched up thirteen concrete steps onto a wide porch with ivy-covered pillars, and handed off to an inside lackey who frisked him a second time, again pretty damned personally, and led him into a sunny atrium the size of a gymnasium. Glass on three sides looked out over the courtyard wall. Seattle was a brown haze across choppy, cold-looking gray water. All the rest of the view was of various kinds of blue or green conifers.

Seidel strolled in, dressed for tennis in a short-sleeved shirt and slacks, wearing white sneakers. He looked like a tennis pro, not large or muscular, but with movie-star features and radiating athletic energy. His brown hair was cut fashionably too long, and he had a suntan that looked expensive in Seattle. The two bodyguards who flanked him stopped in the doorway and stood with their hands inside their jackets, surly stone pillars closely related to Ivan.

"You wanted to talk, so talk." Seidel opened a cabinet, took out a glass, held it under an ice dispenser and sloshed in vodka. He motioned for Jossef to help himself. Jossef leapt to the cabinet and savored the sweet rewards of success, real vodka in an unmarked bottle, straight from Russia.

Jossef tried the "old times" routine, but Seidel had no memory of ever having been in Miami, although he managed a salacious grin when Jossef mentioned the whips.

Seidel understood the exigencies of war, and was happy to lend a beleaguered fellow Capo twenty soldiers for a couple of weeks, for a fee, or course.

"Shall we say $5,000 each per week, payable two weeks in advance?"

Jossef looked at the bodyguards, who were standing like a couple of Doric pillars by the doorway with their hands sort of twitching inside their jackets. He guessed it was not a time to haggle, and a little late to back out of the deal. He extended his hand for a hearty handshake, and got a clap on the back from the great man himself.

Seidel handed Jossef a business card that had only a phone number on it.

"If you need to keep the soldiers longer, you can just call this number." He took the card back, dug a notebook out of his pocket, and penciled in the number of an American Express office. "If anything comes up, you can send the payment in advance there," he explained.

Seidel nodded to the two guards by the door. In the next second, Jossef was blindfolded and being shoved down the outside stairs. When his blindfold was removed, he was standing in the parking lot at the Edgewater. An accountant type who had been riding in the jump seat knocking knees with Jossef accompanied him to his room and accepted two hundred thousand cash from Jossef's carry-on bag.

The 727 to Anchorage was packed, with twenty of the passengers on the rowdy side, demanding vodka, complaining about the Smirnoff, and becoming belligerent when the supply ran out. Three guys in the front seats had snared a bit more than their fair share of the vodka, and one of them discovered that a passing flight attendant had very nice soft buns.

He shared that information with his seatmates, so the next time she came by, they scooped her up and laid her across the three seats to verify that information. They found she had other nice attributes, too, and were in the process of baring those for better evaluation. Another attendant burst out of the galley with a bottle of seltzer water and sprayed it back and forth in the miscreants' faces until the object of their affection had wriggled free, abandoning most of her clothes, and run screaming into the cockpit.

That might have caused serious trouble, but the three Lotharios were too drunk to get their seat belts open and almost instantly forgot the incident, anyway. When the plane stopped at the gate in Anchorage, passengers were told to remain seated while a small army of federal marshals stormed aboard and helped the sagging Russians off the plane. Jossef watched in dismay while $30,000 worth of beef, as he saw them, were hustled away, probably for three-to-five in a federal prison.

Wien Air couldn't fit the seventeen remaining soldiers and Jossef onto the next flight. Jossef had to decide whether it was safer to go ahead himself and trust the rest to follow, or to send a dozen soldiers ahead to wait for him in Fairbanks. He noted several thousand dollars worth of his beef eyeing the Alaska Airlines desk where a return flight to Seattle was queuing up, so he sent the dozen who looked like the greatest flight risks on ahead to Fairbanks, and settled down in the bar to buy vodka for the remaining five while they waited two hours for the next Fairbanks flight.

The five soldiers who deplaned with Jossef in Fairbanks had become pretty mellow and were helping each other into the terminal building. A fuss was going on at the main entrance and eight of Jossef's soldiers were watching with interest, hands in pockets. One of their compatriots was being handed off by airport security to the Fairbanks city police.

Jossef asked what the problem was, and the soldiers didn't quite understand themselves. All the guy had done was fall in love with an Athabascan beauty who was running the information booth. She had led him on with a friendly smile, but when he wanted to start their family right away, inside the booth, she had called security, and they had taken her side of the argument.

Jossef looked around and seemed to be missing a few heads. "Oh, them," he was informed, "they didn't like Fairbanks so they got back on the plane right after we got off."

Passengers were queuing up for the return flight to Anchorage and Jossef spotted two more of his men in that line. He realized that he may have become a little soft, but he still remembered how to be a Capo.

He charged the line, scooping up a stool as he passed, and laid both deserters out cold on the floor. The queuing passengers stepped back, compatriots dragged the unconscious warriors to the doors, passengers filled in the gap in the line, and the little army marched, or were dragged, with the recent Anchorage arrivals being supported on shoulders, out into the anemic Fairbanks sunshine. Fourteen soldiers and Jossef piled into waiting taxicabs for the trip to the fortress on Chena Ridge.

The realities of keeping an army came fully home to Jossef when his crew charged the empty refrigerator and the howl could probably be heard down in Fairbanks. Jossef called Godfather's Pizza for two dozen large combinations and sent Yuri scrambling down the hill in the Mercedes for two cases of that Stolichnaya piss. Speaking of piss, the mansion had only three bathrooms, so most of his new soldiers were relieving themselves off the balcony, running a contest to see who could make it to the river.

The door to his office had been jimmied. He moved the desk and the pad. There were several dents in the knob on his safe, so he had to go to the kitchen for a pair of pliers to open it, but his stash was all there.

When the crew finally settled down among the empty pizza boxes to nurse their bottles of Stolichnaya for the night, Jossef surveyed the scene with some satisfaction. This was just like the old days, except . . . except, he realized to his horror that he didn't see any weapons. The airline passengers hadn't carried any arsenals in their bags.

Jossef had four Kalashnikovs. Boris, Ivan and Yuri each had their Glocks, and of course Jossef had stuck his Colt .45 in his belt the moment he found it still in the desk drawer in his office, and he had every intention of keeping it handy. He ran back to his office, placed an emergency call to the number that Seidel had given him. Seidel was all cooperation and sympathy. He agreed to ship a dozen Kalashnikovs express airfreight for $10,000 each.

Joseph screamed the anguished cry of a wounded animal. "I can buy Kalashnikovs for $2,000 each in Brooklyn."

"Well, of course that is your option. If you wish to spend a few days shopping around, you go right ahead. I'm just telling you what the rifles are worth to me."

Joseph started a growl that ended in a sob, and Yuri went careening down the mountain in the Mercedes to American Express with $120,000 to send, and $1,200 for the fee. Two days and seventy-two pizzas later, the rifles arrived. Jossef called Checker Cab and chartered a bus for a trip to Anchorage. He opted to save the expense of a driver. He could drive the bus himself.

Chapter 12

Pauline called the meeting to order, this time wearing a blue jumper, still no blouse. Renaldo was sitting back in the shadows, but he had put some kind of makeup over his burns, so he didn't look too bad. Renaldo and I were sort of heroes, having survived, if not exactly repulsed, an all-out attack by the Russians. We had four more kibitzers from the out-of-town set, and our original board of directors was starting to look pretty confident, maybe professional.

"I understand that Wyatt Earp has been moonlighting as Sherlock Holmes, so how about a report, Sherlock?" She turned to me, and her disdain wasn't quite so noticeable as it had been. I stood up and addressed the group.

"What I think I just might have found out is what Schneider tried to tell us at our first meeting. The Russians rented their car Thursday night, half an hour after a jet arrived from Fairbanks, but before the evening jet came in from Seattle. They turned the car in at 9:00 Friday morning, just after a jet left for Seattle, but forty-five minutes before a flight for Fairbanks. I think the Russkie's headquarters is in Fairbanks and all we're getting here are ambassadors." I sat down, and quite a few heads were nodding.

"Okay," Pauline seemed to take my report as fact. "Do we go after them, or wait for them to come to us?"

"Wish I still had my bazooka," Alvarez growled. "I'd be all for smoking them out of their lair." Alvarez wore a belligerent expression that emphasized his hawkish features and looked the way I think South American mercenaries look on the evening before a coup.

Pinky stood up and ran his hands through his great thatch of gray hair. "The first rule of war is to know your enemy. That's what Special Forces were all about, and it's still true. I think we should send Sherlock Holmes to Fairbanks to reconnoiter the situation." He sat back down, but I was already on my feet.

"No, nix, nein, nada, nyet, no way. Your reconnoiter idea is right on, but I'm not the one to do it. I know where the Fairbanks bars are, but they don't know me, and nobody is going to talk to me. Don't some of you old-timers have some contacts up there?"

That brought a round of buzzing private conferences, and pretty soon some gray heads were nodding. Then a flaming red one slammed her glass down on the table.

"Sherlock is right, for a change. I know that kid who was in the bar where the Russkies first blew away the cops because his momma used to work for me. Still would be if that dredge man hadn't dragged her off to Ester."

That brought more confessions, and the only ones at the conference table who weren't nodding were me, Renaldo, and Schneider. I had noticed that Renaldo's two bottles of Cutty Sark were getting pretty low, so it was a good idea to wrap the meeting up early. I stood up.

"I have a Cessna 310 standing by at Merrill Field. I can take six passengers to Fairbanks, right now if you want to go."

"What?" Pauline was scandalized. "Get to Fairbanks in time for breakfast? Forget it, sonny, our business is with the bar owners and they don't come out of their holes until evening. I say we should get there around six o'clock to-morrow afternoon, you can buy us some lunch, and we'll hit the bars by eight or nine."

I looked around the table. Alvarez was nodding, Rohrbaugh looked like Christmas morning, Harry toasted me with his scotch, Avram whipped out an imaginary pistol and shot me between the eyes. Pinky gave me a wink, started to smile, snapped his lips shut while he readjusted his teeth, then completed a happy grin.

"Okay," I said, "we'll take off from Wilbur's Flight Service at four tomor-row afternoon." I noticed some head shaking and some grimaces from the peanut gallery, but none of them had anything to say. Pauline did.

"Let's get some sleep. Meeting adjourned." She put her usual stamp on the finale by draining her glass, slapping it down on the table, and standing up.

When I stepped into the room, Maggie seemed to be panting. I ran around the bed to rip the drapes open and get some light, and since I was there, I shoved the glass door to the balcony open, just in case she was drowning in the alcohol fumes. When I turned around, there was not one, but two, heads on the pillows. They were both breathing normally, but out of sync.

The new girl looked familiar, but I couldn't put a name or a village to her. She did put me in mind of the coast, so maybe she was from Quinhagak or Goodnews Bay. Her hair was shorter than Maggie's, but still quite a lot was spread out on the pillow, and her breasts were enormous. She was lying on her back, so they were kind of splayed out to the sides, and the nipples were more like those miniature gumdrops than Maggie's pencil erasers.

I decided not to pull the comforter up; it was too dangerous. Maggie was in the center of the bed, but there was still enough room for me. I crawled in, resolutely facing the window. The new girl was almost certainly a cousin of Maggie's, and of course Maggie was sharing.

At 3:59 the next afternoon, I was standing on the wing of the 310 with the door open. Pauline's Cadillac whipped into the lot and slid to a stop in a cloud of dust. Two minutes later, Rohrbaugh and Harry came tooling up in a Toyota and parked next to Pauline. Her Cadillac made the Toyota look like a toy, but the two guys who climbed out, wearing clean plaid shirts and clean jeans, were real. Rohrbaugh was in the passenger seat with the seat all the way back and his knees up even with his chest. Harry was driving, and when he got out I noticed that he'd been sitting on a pillow.

A taxi pulled off the street and stopped two feet from the plane. Pinky climbed out of the front seat and paid the driver; Alvarez and Avram got out of the back, waving bills. Pinky gave them a deprecating gesture and they put their money away.

There didn't seem to be any argument. Pauline got the copilot's seat, so she got in last. I locked the door, cranked the engines, and called for permission to taxi. Most of the traffic was using the short, north-south runway. That's a dirt strip that crosses the main paved runway three hundred feet from the near, or west, end. That would have been a long taxi for us, and maybe the tower operator had seen us load. He directed me to the main paved strip for a takeoff to the east. A Piper Cherokee took off and crossed in front of us. An Aeronca sedan landed and turned off short of our runway, and we were cleared to go.

I know I'm supposed to be jaded, but it is a thrill when two big engines speak in unison, and maybe I was catching some excitement from my passengers. I did feel a little like a kid on an adventure when we broke ground halfway down the strip. I stowed the gear, retracted flaps, and let the 310 show its stuff until we hit two thousand feet. We made a left turnout, away from the shimmering, sun-drenched Chugach Mountains, and followed Ship Creek to the edge of Cook Inlet.

It took a few seconds to set up a cruise while our speed built to 170 knots, then fine tune the power so the two engines made a single tone. If you take off from Merrill Field, you have to cross Knik Arm at two thousand feet because traffic from International will be above you and float traffic for Spenard Lake will be below you. All are squeezed down until you pass the approach end of Elmendorf Air Force Base; then the sky's the limit, so to speak.

Our route was right up the Susitna Valley, so I stayed low for the views of Wasilla, Big Lake, Willow, the railroad, and the new highway. A lot of cars, campers, and the occasional bus were scooting below us toward Anchorage. Every lake had speedboats and water skiers zipping around it. We met a train coming down from Fairbanks, sleek, blue with gold trim, and with glass observation domes on every other car. A big silver bus in the distance caught my attention because it seemed to be swerving all over the road. When it got closer, I could see that it was hogging the centerline and forcing cars to dodge on both sides. It was moving about twice as fast as the traffic flow.

The bus was one of the big tour sorts that looked capable of devouring passenger cars. A charter for sure at this time of year. I wondered if there was a medical emergency, maybe a heart attack, or one of those mass poisonings that happen in passenger jets. I supposed a bus that size has a radio on board, so maybe they were meeting a Medivac helicopter in Willow.

The 310 was chewing up the valley fast. Ten minutes out of Talkeetna, I hauled the yoke back, added power, and headed for fifteen thousand feet. Mt. Denali passed on our left wingtip, snow sparkling in the sunshine. I should say that it looked like an ivory tower, but it always reminds me of a vanilla ice cream sundae with a little chocolate running down here and there. Your first close up and personal look at Denali is a shock, because it isn't the broad picturesque mountain that Sydney Lawrence painted. Lawrence painted what he saw, but what he saw was a whole group of mountains.

The broad profile we think of as Denali starts with Mt. Foraker, 17,400 feet; South Buttress, 15,885 feet; East Buttress, 14,700 feet; Mt. Hunter, 14,573 feet; and Browne Tower, 14,530 feet.

It tapers off on the north end with Mt. Silverthrone. The only reason I know Silverthrone is that I put some radio engineers on top with a ski plane once, but it is the size of Washington state's Mt. Rainier. McKinley itself, called Denali, the tall one, by the Athabaskans, is a misshapen spire, 20,320 feet, reminiscent of the Matterhorn. You can fly up glaciers right through the middle of what Lawrence painted.

We headed across the tail of the mountains where they had tapered down to twelve thousand feet. The FAA facility at Summit Lake was off to our right, lake and runway shimmering in sunshine. We could see the railroad and the highway making their turns to go through Windy Pass, but we were shortcutting that. I looked back to check on my passengers because fifteen thousand feet without oxygen is pushing the limit, but no one was panting. I unclipped the little oxygen bottle from under my seat anyway. Pauline waved it away, so I passed it back. Those were not spring chickens back there.

Dall sheep were sunning themselves on a rock ledge and raised their big curled horns to watch us. We passed over the dirt strip and log lodges at Denali, or McKinley, National Park, more mountains, then the deep valley with the Usibelli and Suntrana coal mines was below us, and the railhead at Healy was to our left.

We passed Mt. Deborah and Hess Mountain off to the east, and broke out into the vast Tanana Valley. I trimmed the nose down and let the speed build to two hundred knots for the final dash to Fairbanks. It struck me that we had been pretty quiet on the way up, but it's that kind of flight. Everyone was glued to a window and struck dumb.

I bought the promised lunch at the Model Café on Second Avenue at 7:30, and all my passengers seemed to have an agenda in mind. We planned to meet back at the cafe around two in the morning. When we stepped out into the street at eight-thirty, Harry and Avram hailed cabs, Pinky, Alvarez, and Rohrbaugh disappeared into the crowd and smoke on Second Avenue, and Pauline turned the other way, to Cushman Street and around the corner toward First Avenue.

I was alone in the middle of Fairbanks. I crossed Second to get away from the crowds. Fairbanks' Second Avenue was like Anchorage's Fourth Avenue, with bars all on one side of the street, but in Fairbanks then the south side of the street was hardware store, jewelry store, furniture store, drugstore, instead of the hole in the ground that limits Fourth Avenue.

I strolled up the quiet sidewalk, across the street from the blaring music and the general din of a thousand celebrating drunks, to the old Nordale Hotel. If you saw the movie "Ice Palace," then you saw that hotel with some phony cloth sign covering the word "Nordale." There are many new hotels in Fairbanks, mostly out around the edges of town, but I was thinking of the budget, not real sure if Renaldo was going to reimburse this junket, and the Nordale did seem to fit with the age of my traveling companions. Besides, it's one block from our rendezvous, and that salved my conscience.

I asked for seven rooms; they had only five, but two of them were doubles so I rented them, walking out with a veritable handful of keys. It was close to nine o'clock, still broad daylight in Fairbanks. It didn't seem quite right to be barhopping, but I had five hours to kill, so I forced myself. The Lacey Street Theater was across from me on the corner, advertising a double header: *The Halls of Montezuma* and *The Shores of Tripoli*. I turned my back on that and ducked into a doorway and up the stairs to the Office Lounge.

The Office was in its summer mode, windows tastefully blacked out so it was a comfortable twilight. A jukebox in back was playing elevator music and young outlaws worked two pool tables. The bar was so quiet that you heard the cue sticks hit the balls, and the crack of the balls set the upper decibel limit. Four guys were scattered down the bar, two obviously working stiffs, concentrating on their beers, and two business types, maybe bankers or preachers, wearing suits and sipping martinis. They were discussing earnestly and seemed to be in agreement, but I did notice that one had two olives in his drink, the other two cocktail onions.

The bar was curved on each end, like half a racetrack, and two women were sitting at the far end with one seat between them. I plunked down at the near end of the oval. A clean-cut kid of a bartender came right over. I ordered Captain Morgan and Coke and he served me Captain Morgan and Coke. I laid a ten on the bar, and he replaced it with three ones. I settled down to wondering about the women at the other end of the bar.

They obviously knew each other but weren't chummy, and I couldn't decide if they were working girls, as in offices or schoolrooms, or working girls, as in ladies of the night. Usually you can tell right away, although it's not really clear exactly how, unless their uniforms are just too blatant. These two were provocative, but not over any boundaries. I wasn't interested in them in a professional way, but I do think that people are the most interesting animals on the planet. The world's oldest profession does have a certain fascination and provides a wealth of insight into people. For instance, a couple of prostitutes came to Bethel one time, maybe thinking they were pioneering virgin territory, so to speak. They nearly starved to death until the Chamber of Commerce took pity and bought them tickets back to Anchorage.

It's not that Bethel men don't indulge, very far from it, as any Anchorage prostitute can tell you, but the transaction requires a degree of anonymity. If you picked up a prostitute in Bethel, half the town would know it before you got back to her room, and the other half of the town would be sitting in the coffee shop at the Kuskokwim Inn, watching you sneak in. If those two ladies gave any Bethel men ideas, then the men took the ideas into Anchorage to indulge them anonymously.

I wonder if that's the reason for the apparent moral decline in society. A century ago, most people lived in small towns or on farms, and the only way to get anonymous was to go out west, so maybe that's even the reason that the west was wild. Today, with most people living in cities and families scattered from coast to coast, everyone is anonymous—at least until they go into politics.

A big guy wearing a flashy sport coat and several rings breezed into the bar. He walked straight to the stool between the two women and sat down. The bartender ran right over with a shot glass of something amber. The guy downed the drink, got up and extended his elbows. Each of the women latched onto an elbow, and the trio marched out. I still wonder what that relationship was.

My drink was gone, and I had killed one of my five hours. The bar wasn't so interesting after the women departed, so I left the three ones on the bar and wandered back down the stairs. I'm no neophyte to Alaska, and I've come out of bars as far north as Point Barrow, both summer and winter, but it's still a shock to step out of a dark bar in the shank of the evening and find bright daylight outside.

The flight from Anchorage to Fairbanks is only three hundred miles, but straight north. The earth is not round like a ball, it's round like a tangerine with flat spots top and bottom, so as you approach the Arctic Circle, even a few miles makes a big difference in the amount of daylight. In Fairbanks, we were a nominal one hundred miles from the Arctic Circle and would soon have twenty-three hours of daylight, while Anchorage and Bethel would top out at twenty-one hours.

I strolled up Lacey Street, past a couple of establishments where foosball seemed to be the main attraction, and turned left on Third into the Northward Building. That old aluminum-covered edifice takes up the whole block and was the model for Ferber's Ice Palace. It has a lot of horror stories to tell, like the flood in fifty-eight when the sewers backed up and the basement filled, right up to and including the lobby floor, with raw sewage. That was particularly tough on the television station that was located in the basement at the time.

The bar in the Northward had a good jazz band going, lots of *gussaks* dancing, and short skirts flying. Most of the walls were mirrors with a shelf and stools ringing the dance floor, so wherever you sat, you seemed to be in the middle of the dancers. I found a stool, and a waitress, wearing mostly mesh hose under a bunny suit with no ears or tail, came to take my order.

I was on my second drink, still contemplating human nature, when a bright young lady in short skirt and stretched sweater came over and smiled at me.

"Hi, care to dance?"

Somehow I had gotten so used to spectating that I had forgotten I was at a party.

"Love to." She caught my hand and pulled me off the stool. We did a passable mambo together, and then a pretty good cha-cha. Naturally, I sat at her table, and naturally bought her a drink. She was a good-looking woman with dainty regular features, early thirties I think, and blonde enough to turn heads.

She toyed with her gin and tonic. "This is really exciting for me; so many beautiful people, and strong handsome men like you. I'm a school teacher from Nenana and it's really quiet there, you know?"

"Yeah, I know. I'm from Bethel myself, so I really don't know how to act in the big city."

"You here on business?" she asked. It was noisy in there, so she had to lean close to hear, and she very naturally rested her hand on my thigh.

"Business related, anyhow. You?"

"Sneaking a few days off. I came up on the train just to see some lights and hear some music. I do love Nenana, and my favorite pastime is reading books beside the Tanana River, but it does get awfully quiet."

The band struck up a fox-trot and we trotted. She seemed to melt against me even more than the slow dance required, and I certainly didn't mind. She had really nice breasts that nestled into my chest deliciously.

Back at the table, we discussed bars, and how there is only one in Nenana, but she was afraid to go in because it was too loud, and people were always getting stabbed and shot in there. That brought a shudder to her slender frame, and she snuggled against me for reassurance. I put a protective arm around her shoulders and appreciated her warm thigh pressed against my leg. I was having visions of protecting this sweet little girl with the soft warm body for the rest of my life, and wondering if she would like Bethel, or if I would have to move to Nenana.

The next number was something I didn't recognize, but it had a disco beat and I got up to dance. She pulled me back into the embrace.

"I've had enough dancing for a while. Why don't you take me up to my room? It's forty bucks for a quickie and three hundred if you want to spend the night."

That put a different slant on things because the Northward Building is not a hotel. Those rooms upstairs are apartments, so if she had one, the schoolteacher persona was suspect. I told her I was terribly sorry but had a prior engagement. She stalked off toward the bar, and a minute later I saw her dancing with another guy. I went outside and hailed a cab. I still had time to fill; the Club Zanzibar, where the Richardson Highway sweeps outside the city limits, can be counted on for music and I'd had enough dancing for awhile.

Fairbanks is like a little model of America. The farther south you go, the darker the population gets, and when you get to the Club Zanzibar, the clientele is pure black. It was dark in there, except for pink and blue spotlights on the stage, and I felt like an albino. When I sat at the bar, sickly Alaskan white, it seemed like there was a spotlight on me.

Right away I forgot feeling conspicuous, because there was a big guy, totally bald, maybe in his sixties and raven black, making passionate love to a tenor saxophone. That sax got right inside me and vibrated my soul. He was belting out the "Lullaby of Birdland" at a floor-shaking hundred decibels. It was like doing aerobatics in a Supercub, dropping your stomach out one second and then going light in the head on the high notes. I was so entranced that when the bartender asked, I ordered Captain Morgan and Coke.

It was Bacardi, but the Coke was real, and I didn't care, as long as that sax kept blowing. He segued straight into "Harlem Nocturne," which was pretty nearly orgasmic. It wasn't until he put the sax down that I noticed there was a keyboard and a bass fiddle involved in the sound. Sachmo took six deep breaths, wiped a gallon of sweat off his head with a big white handkerchief, and jumped right into "Bad, Bad, Leroy Brown." No one was singing, but it didn't matter; he was doing the lyrics on the saxophone.

A very nicely shaped silver lamé gown sparkled out of the dark and snuggled up to me. The gown plastered breasts against my back and interesting curves all the way down to the bar stool.

"Wanna buy me a drink, handsome?" Her voice came from the same planet that had exported the sax.

My only excuse is that there was nothing in my head except the music. I said, "Sure, why not?" She said, "Champagne cocktail." The bartender said, "Twenty dollars."

That broke the spell. The bartender was standing expectantly with his hand out, and I think I recognized him; I think he was a fullback for the Green Bay Packers. I dug a twenty out of the roll in my pocket and handed it over. The smile tilted what was obviously a champagne glass full of ginger ale, and downed it in one swallow.

She came around to sit almost in my lap, her hand trailing accidentally down into what was definitely my lap.

"Wanna buy me another?" she asked.

I gave her a friendly swat on an ample bottom, said "Later," and she drifted away. I got back into the music.

Maybe I should explain that I never carry money in my wallet. The wallet has licenses and credit cards, and is just too important to be dragging out of your pocket. You definitely don't want someone to see you stuffing bills in there. I keep my wallet buttoned in my back pocket and carry bills, if any, rolled in my left front pocket. Keys, pocketknife, whatever else, go in the right front pocket, so I'm not going to be dropping money when I dig out my keys.

The band took a break, but the jukebox filled the void at the same volume. The spotlights began to strobe, all colors, and a giant peacock leapt onto the stage. Someone announced that we should give a big hand to Princess Zenobia, and we did.

The peacock began to dance, a relative of the striptease, but with a definite African slant to it, a rhythm that conjured up steaming jungles, intrigue, and voodoo rituals. Feathers flew. Some were plucked off in chunks and tossed backstage, others just floated away from the sheer exuberance of the dance.

As the feathers thinned, the most sinuous, sensuous, voluptuous, exotic female body I have ever ogled emerged, until the final feather was gone. One beat later the princess was gone, too. We clapped and pounded the bar, whistled and shouted, and I was right in there, pounding my palms and screaming my lungs out.

The princess stepped back into the light in all her naked glory for one half a heart-thump, and the lights went out. It was so dark in that bar that my luminous watch dial got my attention and it read one-thirty. The lights came on, no longer strobing, the jukebox came up a little mellower. The princess was as gone as a wet dream. My wait was over, and I hurried outside to grab a cab.

Chapter 13

Jossef was hunched like a madman over the wheel of the big bus. He had left Fairbanks doing seventy miles per hour, but that was six hours ago, and he kept driving faster, as though he might get away from the racket going on behind him. The bus had a tendency to swerve back and forth whenever a major fight broke out, but it was worse when they launched into a Russian folk song. They all swayed in unison, and the bus swerved to the rhythm. Driving the swaying bus felt like riding a bicycle. They came across the bridge over Hurricane Gulch, looking down five hundred feet at the river and rocks, and using both lanes to keep the bus from tipping over.

The bus was doing eighty-five now. Jossef found that traffic was not a problem if he just straddled the yellow line, kept one hand on the horn, and let the cars dodge into the ditches on either side. The valley was getting wider, but the damn mountains were still right there on both sides. A twin-engine plane ripped by overhead toward Fairbanks, and he cursed himself for not thinking to charter a plane. If he had chartered, they could have carried all the guns they wanted, and they would already be in Anchorage.

Jossef patted the .45 in his belt and consoled himself with the thought of what he was going to do to the Italians at the Malamute Saloon. The highway made a sweeping turn to the left, the mountains on the right dropped away, and he noticed that it was getting dark. How the hell could that be? He'd been told that it wouldn't get dark until the end of August.

By the time Anchorage grew up around them, he had headlights on and was leaning on the horn most of the time just to keep his speed up to sixty. Yuri, wearing his felt hat low over his ears, was standing in the door-well to direct. He grabbed for the handle to hold himself in when Jossef swung wide to use both lanes and screeched around the corner off E Street onto Fourth Avenue. The taxi that was turning onto E took to the sidewalk, people scattered, and the bus shuddered to a halt, blocking the three taxi stands that happened to be vacant in front of the Malamute Saloon.

Jossef swung the door open, whacking the sign that read, "Taxi Zone, Tow Away," and soldiers began staggering out onto the sidewalk. They looked more like the aftermath of a war than the beginning of one, but they were jamming clips into rifles and loading rounds. Yuri charged through the open bar door into a dark haze of smoke and alcohol fumes and two hundred dancers who were "Rollin', rollin', rollin' on de river."

Renaldo, behind the bar, recognized Yuri and dropped to his knees before Yuri could return the compliment. The other bartenders closed ranks above Renaldo and kept right on opening beers. Greg, leading the band, had a view over the bar and saw a steady stream of soldiers crowding through the door, waving rifles. Greg reached down to the amplifier and cranked the volume to max. He whacked his guitar, the rafters shook, and the dancing stopped.

"One, two, Oh when the Saints, go marching in . . ." The band members stepped to their microphones, and two hundred people belted out the lyrics along with the band, clapping and stomping the rhythm. The sound waves were a live thing, swinging the chandeliers and bulging the walls.

Yuri shouldered his way through the crowd, Jossef right behind him, .45 in hand, the rest of the troops fanning out into a flying wedge. The crowd parted to let them through, but never took its eyes off Greg. "Oh Lord, I want to be in that number . . ." Yuri led the soldiers straight to the closed office door and reached to open it. Jossef jerked Yuri's hand back.

Greg gestured with his guitar, dividing the room into two halves, and pointed to the left half. "Oh when the Saints." Right half, "Oh when the Saints", left half, "go marching in."

Jossef motioned to Ivan. Ivan stepped up to the door and cut loose with his Kalashnikov, wiping it slowly back and forth across the door, angling to both sides to cover the room inside.

"Oh Lord, I want to be in that number." Pow, pow, pow. "When the saints go marching in." Pow, pow, pow. Left half, "Oh when the Saints." Pow, pow. Right half, "Oh when the Saints." Pow, pow, "go marching in."

Ivan emptied his rifle. The door was completely cut in half above the latch, and the top half swung open, hanging dangerously from one hinge. Instead of the expected room full of Italian gore, there were rows of bullet holes in cement blocks behind a vacant desk.

Jossef spotted the back door and realized that the Italians must have run out that way. He screamed, "Follow me," but Boris, a foot away, couldn't hear him. "Oh Lord, I want to be in that number . . ." Jossef waved a "follow me" with his .45 and ripped the bolts open on the back door. They came out shooting, but the alley was deserted . . . except for one vehicle, that most Italian of all cars, a lipstick-red Alfa Romeo.

Thunder erupted in the alley. Soldiers shot the Alfa from all sides, leaning in to shoot the dash, making rows up and down the seats, blasting off fenders. Jossef ran around the car, blowing out lights with his .45. Shooting the tires wasn't enough; they swept around and around the tires until they were nothing but rags. The hood had popped open and a hundred rounds were bounced off the engine. Shooting began to taper off as rifle after rifle was emptied.

The back door to the bar had swung shut. Jossef jammed fingers into the gap and pulled, but the door was locked from the inside. He stepped back two feet and finished emptying his automatic at the door, then hit the dirt while the bullets bounced off the steel door and ricocheted back and forth across the alley.

Suddenly it was almost silent, except for the steel door that had stopped vibrating to the gunshots and was vibrating to, "Oh Lord, I want to be in that number . . ."

Jossef stood up and brushed at the mud on his clothes. He waved for Yuri. "Give me some more ammunition."

"It's in the bus," Yuri squeaked, realizing that wasn't good, but unable to remember having been put in charge of ammunition.

That was too much. Jossef jerked up the automatic to shoot Yuri's ears off, but the hammer clicked on an empty chamber. "Well, go get it," Jossef screamed. The soldiers were pulling empty clips out of rifles. Yuri ran down the alley to E Street and around the corner. Jossef followed him and the soldiers strung out behind, slogging down the alley past the sagging and smoldering Alfa.

Yuri didn't come back. Jossef rounded the corner onto Fourth Avenue to see Yuri standing in the middle of the street, doing a frantic series of jumping jacks, and the bus, being towed by a wrecker, disappearing onto C Street two blocks away.

A taxi was sitting smugly in the newly vacated taxi stand and Jossef jumped into it. "Follow that bus," he shouted. He realized he was waving the empty automatic and shoved it into his belt. The taxi driver peeled out, barely missing the leaping Yuri, and screeched after the bus. The driver had got the message that was implicit in the .45.

After six blocks of suicidal maneuvering, the taxi was right behind the bus, blinking lights and blowing horn, but the bus continued implacably down Fifth Avenue and turned left through a gate in a cyclone fence. The gate slammed shut, and the taxi skidded to a stop with its bumper against the mesh.

Jossef jumped out and shook the gate. It rattled and clanged, but wasn't going anywhere. To his left, at the end of the fence, sat a little office building with the door open and light streaming out. Jossef charged into the office and demanded the return of his bus. Jossef was pounding the desk with his fists and shouting, but the little Native girl facing him seemed unperturbed. Three men sat at desks around the room, typing forms.

"I'm sorry, sir, there's a traffic ticket on that bus. The ticket will have to be paid before we can release the bus."

Jossef jerked the automatic out of his belt, forgetting for the moment that it was empty. He started to scream his request again, waving the .45 in her face, but he felt a strange electricity in the air. He glanced around the room. All three guys had stopped typing and each held a double-barreled shotgun leveled at Jossef. They weren't particularly excited; apparently a little gun waving was standard for Alaskans with impounded cars.

Jossef swept his eyes around the room again; none of the shotguns had wavered. He jammed the automatic back into his belt.

He struggled, gulped down air, and got himself under control. "Okay, how much is the ticket?"

"It will be fifty dollars for the ticket and a hundred dollars for the tow, sir."

Jossef pulled a couple of stray hundred-dollar bills out of his jacket pocket and pushed them across the desk.

"Oh, I'm sorry, sir. You can't pay the ticket here. That has to be paid at the police station, after eight o'clock in the morning. When you have the release from the police, then you come back here and pay for the tow, and we can release the bus."

Two of the guys had gotten out of their chairs to sit comfortably on their desks, shotgun barrels unwavering from Jossef's chest. He choked down bile, spun around, and stomped out the door. As an afterthought, he grabbed the door and slammed it shut. The glass panel in the door shattered, and that was some consolation.

The taxi dropped Jossef back at Fourth and E, but he didn't see his army anywhere. His head was starting to ache; his hatred for the Italians almost boiled his blood. He noticed a row of rifle barrels leaning inside the window in the first bar. He covered his ears and held his aching head with his hands. He glanced into the bar through the wide-open door.

When his eyes adjusted to the haze, he could see several of his soldiers dancing and Yuri sitting at the end of the bar, nursing a drink. Yuri had his hat pulled all the way down over his ears and sat with his elbows on the bar, his hands pressing the hat tighter. Jossef recognized a companion headache, and a wave of affection for the faithful Yuri washed over him. Suddenly Jossef's head felt better. He stomped in, sat down next to Yuri, and ordered vodka.

By three in the morning, the music had tapered off and the army began to reassemble. They came staggering out of bars all along the street, including a few from the Malamute, most towing their empty rifles by the barrels with the butts dragging on the sidewalk. Jossef leaned against the lamppost on the corner and tried to count, but his brain wouldn't cooperate. He seemed to be missing a few, but couldn't remember how many he was supposed to have. Two very Russian-looking guys came out of the Silver Dollar down the street, but they weren't dragging rifles. Each had a girl on his arm, and both turned the other way and meandered away toward D Street.

Jossef's brain wrestled with that problem and finally remembered that the rifles had cost him $10,000 apiece. He motioned to Yuri. Yuri stood up from his seat on the sidewalk, where he had been leaning comfortably against the wall, and wove his way down to the Silver Dollar, running his hand along the building fronts to hold himself up. He came back out in a couple of minutes, towing two Kalashnikovs by the barrels.

A big guy with a handlebar mustache came out of the Malamute, locked the door, and when he turned around, bumped into Yuri. Yuri staggered. There was something familiar about that guy, but Yuri needed to concentrate on walking. The guy marched down Fourth, nodded to Jossef at the corner of E Street, swept around the corner, and continued to the alley. There was a horrible scream from the alley, but Jossef supposed the guy was just being mugged. He turned and wearily led his platoon down Fourth Avenue, away from the carnage.

At the corner of Fourth and G, he spotted a hotel jutting up on Fifth Avenue and turned the corner. He counted twelve men, so rented six rooms. Yuri, who was going to be Jossef's roommate, stood expectantly, cradling the two salvaged rifles in his arms. Suddenly Jossef wanted to be alone. He handed the room key to Yuri and stumbled into the coffee shop.

Chapter 14

I straggled into the Model Café at five minutes before two. The crew was assembled, and darned if they didn't look thirty years younger than they had yesterday. They were just ordering breakfast, and I rushed to join them. Pauline ordered brains and eggs, but that didn't catch on. I settled for hash and scrambled. The waitress left, and a pandemonium of reports broke out.

It took some sorting, but the general consensus was that the Russian army was a hoax. No one in Fairbanks had ever seen anyone except the Ed Asner guy, and Pauline iced the cake. The bartender on First Avenue, the one who originally reported the twenty soldiers, had succumbed to Pauline's maternal persuasions and admitted that there was just one old guy with a rifle and a nice bribe for him to make up the extra soldiers.

Avram had the information that a liquor store belonging to a friend of his used to deliver twelve bottles of Stolichnaya to a mansion up on Chena Ridge every week, but the order dropped to only eight fifths a week right after the car fire in Anchorage. It didn't take much math to come up with only three or four Russians up there.

"And they know where this mansion is?" I asked.

"Sure do, I've got a marked map right here in my pocket." Avram proudly pulled out a Fairbanks city map with a big X marking a spot on Chena Ridge Road.

Pauline's "brains and eggs" was a scrambled affair with little cubes of white or pink in it that looked like cheese.

"So," Pinky wanted to know, "shall we go up there and blast them?" A blob of whipped cream from his strawberry waffle had escaped onto his cheek. His tongue came out and snared the errant morsel.

"Hey, not too fast here, don't forget they've got guns. Maybe we can just drive by and get a look at the place." I was backpedaling, but remember, I had just seen what a Kalashnikov can do to a parking lot.

"So, who hasn't got guns?" Rohrbaugh asked. He dug in his pants pocket and pulled out a Derringer, over/under two shot, and slammed it on the table. My heart sank, but Pinky reached in the back of his pants and came out with a .45 automatic, probably left over from WW II. The race was on. Harry plunked a .38 Patrolman on the table, Pauline reached into a skirt pocket and added a .22 caliber High Standard revolver to the pile, and more were coming out. My heart wasn't sinking anymore; it was sunk. I had my .357 in my jacket pocket, of course, unfortunately still loaded with .38s, but it felt pretty small at that moment.

"We'll talk about it tomorrow," I said. I grabbed the check and headed for the cash register. The guns were disappearing off the table, back into their nests.

We walked down the street toward the Nordale, still on the north side, passing bars until we came to the Union Club and a body came flying out the door and slammed into Pinky. A little Indian gal was right behind the body, cursing and screaming at it, and when she started kicking it in the ribs, we all had to dodge. We crossed to the drugstore side of the street.

At the Nordale, we paused in the lobby while I handed out keys. The single rooms were on the second floor, the doubles on the first floor, so I handed Pauline the key to 201 and fanned out the rest of the keys, inviting everyone to draw straws. Harry and Pinky drew the two first floor keys, and Rohrbaugh did a double take when he realized there were no more keys.

"It's okay," I told him, "you're bunking in a double with Harry. Pinky, looks like I'm in with you."

"Meet around nine?" Pauline suggested. General nods and exeunt.

Pinky was in the bathroom quite a while and came out wearing striped boxer shorts and carrying a glass of water with his teeth reposing in it. I took my turn, and when I came out, Pinky was snoring in the bed by the window. I got the bed by the door. Pinky's rendition was definitely masculine, not much like Maggie's purr, but it was regular and not unpleasant. It was like going to sleep listening to ocean surf.

Pauline called the morning meeting to order over after-breakfast coffee at the Model Café.

"I vote that we drive up and have a look. Sherlock, go get us some cars."

Pauline did have a way of taking unanimous votes. I hiked down the now quiet, safe Second Avenue to Lacey Street and turned left for one block to the Polaris Building. Hertz didn't have anything that would haul seven passengers, so I rented a pair of Dodge Darts. The cars were across First Avenue in a parking lot between the street and the Chena River. I took both sets of keys and drove one car back to the Model, where the crew was standing expectantly on the sidewalk. Pauline rode back to Hertz with me to get the second car. Then Avram climbed in front beside me, proudly unfolding his map, and twenty minutes later we'd passed the college and made twin dust plumes up Chena Ridge Road.

The Tanana Valley spread out on our left, a maze of lakes, meadows, bogs, woods, and creeks, flat for thirty miles to the foot of the snow-covered Alaska Range. Here and there, you could see two white dots on a lake: swans that were nesting and big enough to be visible for miles. On our right, the yellow-green of new leaves on willows, poplars, and birch trees covered hills that stretched away into a purple haze. A sprinkling of snow still left on Ester Dome dominated the panorama.

Avram had his finger on the map and was watching the odometer.

"There," he crowed, pointing to a driveway that led down into woods on our left.

I slowed down, but continued on for a hundred yards to a turnout and a spot that would be labeled *Scenic View* someday after the road was paved.

We piled out of the cars and looked at each other uncertainly, but Pinky had no doubts. He whipped out his .45, held it high, and charged down the hill into the woods. We followed, guns appearing from pockets and belts as we went. The ground under the trees was hard, a lot of it bare rock, and the dead leaves were too soggy to crackle. Pinky suddenly hunkered down and made get-down motions. We fetched up behind him at a berm where a parking lot had been cleared below us.

The parking lot was gravel, forty feet across, with a Mercedes sedan the only occupant. The house was a big, brown-shake affair that I think should be called ranch style, single story, lots of glass, many different angles to the roof. At a couple of places we could see right through the house, windows in back matching windows in front. I figured the parking lot side below us to be the back, and the patch of green lawn beyond the house, which ended with a drop to the river far below, to be the front. Mostly the house was very dark and still.

"Reckon anyone's at home?" Pinky wondered.

"Must be," Harry pointed out. "The car is there."

"Let's just watch a while." I suggested, "After all, this is a reconnaissance trip."

We settled down on the leaves, peeking over the berm, and waited.

Birds chirped. Two squirrels chased each other out of a spruce tree and scampered around the house. A gray jay—justly called a camp robber—swooped onto the porch and strutted up and down, poking its dagger beak into the cracks between the boards.

"Ain't nobody home." Pinky decided.

"Let's find out." Harry dug a little rock out of the berm and tossed it. It clunked against the door and rattled across the porch. We all ducked down behind the berm. The camp robber squawked indignantly and flew away. Nothing else happened, so Harry chunked another rock that pinged off the picture window. Next thing I knew, a regular barrage of pebbles was being tossed, rattling all over the house; no response came from inside.

"Like I said, ain't nobody home." Pinky stood up, stepped over the berm, and slid down an eight-foot bank into the parking lot. He walked right over to the Mercedes, jerked the door open, and blasted several short beeps on the horn. When that brought no response, I decided he must be right. We clambered over and slid down, maybe like an assault wave on an inverted beachhead.

The door from the porch was locked. Harry trotted around the house and one minute later he opened the door from the inside.

"Back wasn't locked," he explained. We trooped into a room that looked as if it had already been ransacked. Piles of boxes and papers were everywhere, with empty bottles strewn like bowling pins after a strike.

"Someone has to keep watch," I cautioned. "If anyone comes down that driveway we all run out the back and down the hill." General nods. Alvarez stationed himself in the doorway, holding an ancient .44 revolver at the ready. The image of a South American mercenary came back strong.

Pauline picked up a box. "For four guys, they sure ate a lot of pizza."

She had a heck of a point there. "Find some sales slips," I suggested. "Maybe this is six months' accumulation."

"I don't think so." Pauline was shaking her lion's mane. "They stink, but not that bad."

"Here's a sales slip." Harry pulled a crumpled piece of paper out from under a coffee table. "Two dozen pizzas delivered by Godfather's yesterday...you don't suppose...?"

"No, I don't suppose," I told him. "Remember, these are Russians."

"Oh yeah. Hey, here's another one." He unfolded and read. "Another dozen delivered, also yesterday."

"So much for four guys. How many do you figure?" Pinky was asking Pauline.

"Couldn't be less than twenty. Look at all the bottles."

Alvarez strolled out of the kitchen holding up another receipt. "Two cases of Stolichnaya, that's twenty-four bottles, delivered day before yesterday, and I don't see no full bottles left nowhere."

"Holy criminy." Harry was losing his cool. "Here's another case delivered yesterday."

"Okay," I said, "we made a minor miscalculation here, but we're in now. Let's search fast and get out."

"What we looking for?" someone asked.

"I don't know, anything with a name on it? Any lists, anything that looks important." We scattered through the house. I checked on Alvarez. He was on duty, .44 pointed up the driveway.

"Hey," I told him, "don't shoot that thing. If anyone comes, just holler and scamper out the back." He nodded. I tromped through the boxes toward a blank door off the living room. The door was locked, but it had been recently jimmied with a crowbar, so I shoved it back against the hinges, the latch cleared the strike plate, and the door swung open. I was standing in an office: desk, telephone, leather swivel chair, only one pizza box and one empty bottle. I checked the desk. There were lists with check marks in the drawer, and the lists read like my barhopping days. There was the Malamute Saloon, no check mark, but a line drawing of a dagger through it.

I stashed the lists in my pocket and shoved the drawer closed. Something fell off the desk with a clunk. I stooped down and found a pair of water-pump pliers, which seemed odd. Then I noticed on the bottom of the drawer was a taped-down note with a series of four numbers on it.

"Hey," I shouted, "there's a safe somewhere. Find it." Several people ran into the office ready to look, but the usual hiding places weren't there, no pictures, no furniture around the walls.

Avram piped up. "Mine is a floor safe under the mat."

I jumped off the mat and ripped it up. A flush floor safe with a seriously dented knob and some cuts from the pliers was nestled underneath. I grabbed the pliers and the note, made the turns, and the safe popped open. I don't mean it just came open, I mean it was stuffed so full that the lid popped open, and bundles of hundred-dollar bills came pouching out.

That brought a chorus of awed exclamations.

"Hey," Pinky hollered, "that's our money."

"Damn straight it is." Pauline ran out of the room and came back with an empty vodka box. She dropped to her knees and started shoveling the dough into the box.

"Looky here." Pinky grabbed a bundle out of the box. He snapped the rubber band off the bundle, and a pile of newspaper clippings dropped out. "This here's my contribution from this month."

"No it isn't," Avram corrected him. "You used the *News.* These are from *Forbes* magazine; this here is my contribution." For a second, it looked like there was going to be a tug-of-war over the worthless bundle.

"Come on, you ninnies, help me here." Pauline's bosom was restricting her reach, there was still more cash in the hole, and her box was full. Pinky knelt and scooped out more; Pauline came running back with another box and knelt next to him. She gave a happy cry and grabbed something off the floor under the desk. She shook a few strands of toilet paper out of the bale and held up a wooden mousetrap for our inspection before she shoved it into her pocket. "This was my contribution. Sorry there's no blood on it."

"I think it's time to go," Pinky suggested.

"Good idea." That was a general chorus.

We trooped out the door and looked up at the bank where we had slid our assault wave. It didn't look likely. Pinky led us around the house, off the lawn into the woods, and we climbed up and around the parking lot. Pinky and Avram were carrying the boxes, and Pauline was puffing right between them.

"Sure is nice to see our money back." It wasn't clear whether Harry was making a statement or asking a question.

"Heck of a lot more here than we ever paid him." Pinky figured.

"Of course," Pauline explained. "That's the interest."

"Hey, you said you never paid him any." That was Avram.

"Well, maybe not in principle, but I'm certainly entitled to interest."

As usual, no one argued with Pauline. We busted out of the woods and leaned, huffing and puffing, against the cars. A breeze ruffled the bills in Pinky's box and a couple started up. Pinky slapped them back down.

"Where do we look for them next?" Pinky asked.

"Look, guys, we were damn lucky that no one was home, and that's the only reason we're still alive. Now we know there's a big Russian army somewhere, and getting out of town fast is our best chance of staying alive to fight over the money. We can turn these cars in at the airport, and I suggest we do it pronto."

For a change, no one argued with me.

Chapter 15

Maggie sat at the counter, dawdling over the last of her steak, and wondering why she felt like crying. It had been a very strange night on Fourth Avenue. For one thing, Pinky wasn't behind his bar, and for the first time ever, when she and her friends trooped down the stairs into the Side Street, Pauline wasn't there shouting to ask if they had any money.

She'd passed the Malamute Saloon several times during the evening and didn't see Alex in his usual seat by the window. She was a little afraid that Alex might have checked out, but surely he wouldn't do that without telling her. Anyway, she still had the room key, so she could charge her steak and eggs to the room.

Maggie wondered if the unusual night foreshadowed the end of her own residency in Anchorage. She'd been here a couple of years now, and for Maggie, this time was perhaps the equivalent of college for *gussak* girls. She was savoring her freedom and what had at first seemed like the endless possibilities for adventure in the big city; but now her life had settled into a routine—same bars, same friends—almost as restrictive as life in Bethel had been.

Maggie knew that at some point she'd get pregnant, and when that happened she'd go back to Bethel and marry one of the boys she'd gone to high school with, one who had a job if she was very lucky. Their first child would be born in six or seven months, adding valuable new genes to the Bethel pool. After that, she would be stuck, having another baby every year or two and living the humdrum life of a Bethel housewife.

That was the point of her time of freedom, now, on the streets of Anchorage. During the long cold winters and the stifling restrictions of motherhood that stretched ahead of her, Maggie would have this adventure to look back on and relive in memory.

She wondered if perhaps, when her children were grown and gone and her husband had been killed in some accident, she might come back to

Anchorage as so many other village women had done, but she would be old then, forty or more. The GIs in the bars wouldn't be so anxious to buy her drinks or slip her twenty dollars for a few moments in a dark booth.

So far, Maggie had been lucky, and she wondered if perhaps it had something to do with her irregular periods. Sometimes she would go for two, even three months without a period, but she never had any other signs of pregnancy. Then she'd have a period, or at least some spotting, and know that her freedom was assured for another few months.

She wondered about Alex, and why he never responded to the invitations she left out for him. She knew that Alex liked girls, and if even half the rumors in the villages were true, he certainly liked Eskimos. Furthermore, Alex had always been a special friend to Maggie. She'd almost let herself dream of marrying Alex, but she knew that could never be. Alex would marry a *gussak* girl, maybe Connie from the district attorney's office, and maybe he'd still smile at Maggie when she was an old lady carrying babies when they met on the streets of Bethel.

Alex had been smiling at her, and patting her on the head, as long as she could remember. Sometimes, when she was a little girl, really down and sick to death of Bethel, Alex would tell her that she was very beautiful and very special, and that had made her life seem exciting. Even when she'd begun to develop womanly curves, and most men had taken to patting her on the fanny or even feeling her shirt to check the progress of her budding breasts, Alex had continued to pat her on the head as though she were still a little girl.

She'd been maybe fourteen or fifteen years old when friends began inviting her to parties. There was always liquor, and sometimes pot, and the crowd seemed to forget that they were stuck in Bethel. Maggie woke up in strange beds, sometimes in a tangle of naked bodies, and often with no memory of having gone to bed. She realized that she was no longer a virgin, and that was nice. It meant that someone at a party had thought of her as an adult.

When Alex saw her on the street the next day after a party, still bedraggled and usually hung over, he would grab her by the shoulders. He held her so that she had to look into his eyes, and sometimes he shook her. He would tell her that she was too beautiful and too special to be wasting her life like that, but how could he think her life was being wasted? She was bringing happiness to her friends, and often, great pleasure to some of the men, and what could be more important than that?

Maggie's family shared the double bed in their tiny bedroom, and occasionally Maggie was awakened by her parents' making love. Those were nice times, and her parents went to sleep so peacefully afterward.

Maggie's very special talent was putting men to sleep, and that's how she paid for her hotel rooms. She knew just which buttons to push to start men snoring. When a single man had a room, usually one of the *gussak* pilots, those were the best times. Some of them were so anxious that they climbed right into the shower with her. She would push their buttons, using soap and warm water to help, and they would stagger out to fall across the beds. Sometimes when she'd finished her own shower and came out, they'd be snoring, right on top of the covers and still wet from the shower.

She always tried to be the first one up in the mornings and slip out of the rooms before the men awakened. If they woke first, they often wanted a double payment, and those were not so nice. For one thing, they smelled bad, and the ritual of finally leaving was awkward. They always promised that they'd meet somewhere that night, but the meetings never happened. She was amazed and puzzled those mornings when she woke and found that Alex had left without disturbing her.

She could almost always find a place to sleep, but it often meant sharing a room with several of her girlfriends, sleeping six or more to a bed and even waking up on the floor. The young servicemen who panted around her and bought her drinks would have kept her forever, but they never had hotel rooms. They always went back to the base in the morning, and if she spent too much time with them, she had to hustle fast to find a bed for herself.

Her first night with Alex, when he'd come into the bathroom during her shower, her heart had stood still, but he just tinkled in the commode and went back to the bedroom. Alex often seemed to have trouble going to sleep, fidgeting and fussing in the bed beside her. She longed to reach over and help him out, but he never seemed to want that. The more trouble he had drifting off, the farther he scooted to his own side of the bed.

For a panicky second, she wondered if she were too old to be attractive to Alex, but that couldn't be. She looked down at her breasts. They stood firm against her blouse, and when she thought about them, her nipples sprang up and pouched out the fabric. The servicemen had been staring at them all night and making clumsy gestures to feel them, so why didn't they do anything for Alex?

Maggie had finished her steak and eggs long ago, and was lingering over her third or fourth refill of coffee. She'd been staring absently into the mirror beside the pie rack, and began to notice that she was watching a man who sat by himself in a booth by the window. He seemed to be very dejected, and probably lonely. She wondered if, like she sometimes did, he was hoping that someone would come by and offer him a bed.

She knew that she had never seen him before, so he probably didn't have many friends in Anchorage. Her heart went out to him, remembering how long the mornings were when she had to wait in the coffee shop until the bars opened at 6 AM. She wondered how Alex would feel about having an extra roommate. He probably wouldn't mind. Alex understood very well the village concept of sharing, and the night that she'd brought her cousin Mildred from Quinhagak home, Alex hadn't said a word.

Alex hadn't even climbed in beside Mildred, which almost any man would have done. Mildred had those gigantic breasts and the big nipples that drove men crazy. Alex had just crawled into his own side of the bed, being very careful not to touch Maggie, who was half on Alex's side of the bed. He had fussed and squirmed for a long time, but had eventually gone to sleep with no help at all.

Maggie wrote "room 1107" on the tab and signed it. She caught the stranger's eyes in the mirror. He was staring with what she thought was desperation. She sauntered over to his booth, swaying her hips and breasts in the way that always brought a couple of extra drinks.

Jossef waved her away—*probably bashful as well as lonely,* she thought. Maggie scooted into the bench beside him, forcing him to move over with the pressure of her thigh.

"Hi, I'm Maggie, and I have a room upstairs. Wouldn't you like to join me for the night?"

Jossef just stared at her, but she read the longing and the loneliness in his eyes. He did have very nice eyes, deep and expressive, and a handsome but mysterious face. She thought he was probably a very sensitive man. Maggie reached down to pat his zipper, and the expected bulge responded nicely. She knew he'd need her help in going to sleep. She picked up his tab, $2 for a cup of coffee, added a $2 tip, and charged it to 1107. She took his hand and pulled him toward the elevators.

When they stepped into the room, Maggie was relieved that Alex wasn't there. She started to unbutton her blouse and headed for the shower, but Jossef grabbed her by the hair and spun her around. He mashed a desperate, whiskery, boozy kiss against her lips and ripped her blouse open, buttons flying.

He picked Maggie up by the waist and tossed her halfway across the room onto the bed. She was still bouncing, amazed at his hunger, when he jumped on top of her and jerked her skirt off. He did indeed need her help in going to sleep, and she helped him eagerly, first out of friendliness, then from self-preservation, but he hammered away, on and on. He would rear back his head and groan his release, but then keep right on, starting over without a pause.

When, at long last, he crumpled onto the bed beside her, Maggie cradled his exhausted face against her breasts and used her hair to wipe the sweat away from his eyes and forehead. She realized his performance was exactly what she had always dreamed that Alex might do. With a happy smile, she also realized that she was sure she was pregnant.

Chapter 16

Jossef woke up with sunshine in his eyes. He threw out an arm to check the bed beside him, but the girl wasn't there. The bathroom door was open. There were a couple of bath towels crumpled on the floor, but no one was in there, either.

"Good thing," he thought. The last thing he needed was a woman slobbering on him in the morning. He dragged himself into the shower; he seemed to be sticky from his navel to his knees. His clothes were in a pile by the bed, but when he picked them up, he gasped from the stench. It was a mélange of sweat, liquor, and cordite that would gag a maggot. He checked the closet.

Freshly laundered pants and shirts were his size. In a dresser drawer, he found a package of black socks and jockey shorts. The jockey shorts were restrictive and uncomfortable compared to the boxer shorts that Russians wore, but he thought maybe American men never got erections in the daytime. He guessed that he'd be safe for several hours. He tossed his dirty clothes into a wastebasket.

He had to go down to the desk to ask which room he was supposed to be in, started for the elevator, but then went back for an extra key and a list of the other rooms he'd rented. Yuri was still sleeping, eyes closed, mouth wide open, still some bruises on his forehead. He struck Jossef as a pathetic excuse for a Russian soldier.

Jossef went into the bathroom, filled the drinking glass with cold water, and threw it in Yuri's face. Yuri came up sputtering and coughing, but grabbed his hat off the floor and covered his bruises. He looked a little better. Yuri hadn't bothered to undress, so he didn't have the problem with smelling his own clothes. He meekly followed Jossef out into the hall.

They tromped down the hall to room number 703 where Jossef banged on the door for several minutes before Boris opened it. Standing there in his boxer shorts, almost reaching the top of the door, but barely blocking the view sideways, he looked more like a stick-man drawing than a human.

"Coffee shop," Jossef growled, and went to 704. He banged for quite a while and kicked the door a few times, but got no response. The same thing happened at 705, 706, and 707. He stormed back down to the desk and got house security to come up and open the rooms. They were empty, except that each had two Kalashnikovs lying on the floor. Yuri followed along, gathering up rifles as they went.

Yuri stood with his armload of rifles while Jossef argued and shouted at the desk clerk. Yuri could see Boris and Ivan through the glass door of the coffee shop, finishing their breakfasts. His stomach growled, but he suspected that breakfast was not on his schedule.

Jossef was pounding the desk, and he screamed when they informed him that 704 through 707 had left 8 AM wake-up calls. They'd charged breakfast to their rooms and left in the airport shuttle bus.

Jossef's hand kept reaching for his automatic, but he couldn't decide whom to shoot. Then he remembered that the automatic was empty and he couldn't get on an airplane with it, so he jerked it out of his belt and tossed it on top of the pile in Yuri's arms. Boris and Ivan wandered out of the coffee shop, picking their teeth. Jossef settled the bill and turned to Yuri.

"The ticket is fifty, the tow is a hundred, and you'll need some gas, so here's two hundred dollars." He stuffed two bills into Yuri's jacket pocket.

"Get the bus and drive it back to Fairbanks." Jossef stomped out the door and climbed into the waiting Airporter, Ivan and Boris right behind him.

The Airporter slipped out of the driveway and turned toward the airport. Yuri walked around behind the desk to the luggage area and dumped his pile of artillery on the floor. He dug a five-dollar bill out of his pocket and tipped the bellman, then sauntered into the coffee shop. After a strawberry waffle, steak and eggs, and a ham omelet, he caught a cab to the police station.

By two in the afternoon, Mr. John Smith from Seattle, with an address in the middle of Elliot Bay, had secured the bus and driven out onto Fifth Avenue, but he didn't turn toward Fairbanks. He turned right on Fifth to Gambell and left, toward Seward. At Dimond Boulevard, he jogged toward the airport. There were three bars that he knew Ivan and Boris hadn't collected from because they were not on Jossef's list. The bar owners were surprised to see him so early in the day, but they had their payments ready. The rumor of a fifty-man Russian army in town and a dozen people killed wasn't lost on them.

Yuri pocketed the fifteen thousand, swung by the Sheffield for a load of artillery, tipped the bellman another five bucks, and turned the bus toward Fairbanks.

When Jossef climbed out of the taxi and found the front door of the house swinging open, he charged straight through to his office, also open, and seriously barked his shin on the open lid of his safe. His scream was first for his shin, then for the empty safe, then for many, many things. He desperately wanted to shoot somebody, but the worthless Yuri still had his automatic. Boris and Ivan decided to hike up the road and check out the spring greenery.

Jossef was appalled at the unscrupulous Italians, coming right into a man's private home and making off with his hard-earned cash. They were barbarians. Nothing was sacred to them. Jossef gnashed his teeth, thinking of all the years of slaving away, scrimping and saving to get a little retirement fund, and now it was gone. And what about his son's college fund? He supposed he had a son, but maybe it was a daughter. He trusted that his mother-in-law had sent her daughter, Denise, at the right time of month. Slapping Denise silly had excited him, so he was in rare form that day. Certainly he had a child, and now, thanks to the perfidy of the Italians, that child could not go to college. Jossef wondered idly if his child still lived in Brooklyn.

He glanced around the room, looking for a Sicilian message, and looked in the safe, half expecting to find a dead fish. Then he remembered that particular Sicilian message meant "sleeps with the fishes" and he did not think his money was sleeping with fishes. He thought it was probably disappearing into a sinkhole in Las Vegas. He did find a little pile of bill-sized newspaper clippings, but they didn't help his mood.

He stomped out of the office, stepped on a vodka bottle, and fell full length into a pile of empty pizza boxes. His left ankle made a snapping sound and excruciating pain shot up his leg. When Boris and Ivan came back, they found Jossef sitting on the couch, rubbing ice cubes over his ankle, and in a really ugly mood.

"Don't you slobs ever clean up anything? Pigs. I'm surrounded by pigs," he shouted. "Look at this place. It's worse than a party at the Kremlin. Get this garbage out of here." Jossef moaned and went back to rubbing ice on his ankle.

Boris and Ivan were relieved at such a simple solution to the mood. They ran back and forth, carrying armloads of empty boxes outside and stacking them in the middle of the driveway. They made a pile four feet high and six feet in diameter. Boris bent to touch his lighter to the pile and went back in to help Ivan with armloads of bottles.

They came back to the porch, laden with empty bottles, and stared in horror at the fire. Pizza boxes were bursting into flames, rising up like hot air balloons, and the gentle breeze Boris hadn't even noticed was plastering the burning boxes against the front of the house. They dropped the bottles on the porch and ran to stomp on the fire, but it was a losing proposition. The fire was already higher than their heads, and the first couple of stomps catapulted flaming boxes onto the shingled roof.

Jossef heard the frantic shouts and came hobbling out onto the porch, expecting Italians and reaching for his still-absent automatic. He stepped on the bottles, did a plié, a high-kick, and dived headfirst off the porch. His arm hurt so badly that he forgot about his ankle. His soldiers rushed to the aid of their fallen leader, but he swiped them away.

"Go call the fire department, you ninnies."

Ivan leapt up onto the porch, took a long ride on the bottles, slammed into the side of the house, then ducked in the door. He was back in a moment, peering out through the smoke that was coming from inside as well as outside.

"What's the number?" He screamed over the crackling flames.

"Nine-one-one, you moron."

"Oh, yeah," Ivan disappeared back into the house, and a puff of flame replaced him in the doorway.

Boris grabbed Jossef under the arms to pull him away from the flames, but Jossef screamed and cradled his right arm. Boris settled for dragging him by the left arm back to the edge of the parking lot. The heat wasn't too bad, so Boris sat down on the ground beside Jossef to watch the fire. The entire front of the house was a solid sheet of flames, so it was obvious that Ivan would not be coming back.

Jossef felt really bad about the loss of his faithful soldier. A few minutes later, when a siren came wailing up the road, he realized that Ivan's last act had been one of heroism. He had bravely faced the inferno to dial the phone and gasped out the message with his dying breath. Jossef wished that he still had some money so he could set up some kind of memorial. Maybe a scholarship in Ivan's memory would be appropriate.

The siren arrived. A bright green truck emblazoned with *Chena Goldstream Volunteer Fire Dept.* slid to a stop. Men in yellow slickers jumped off the back of the truck, jerked out hoses and began wetting down the trees all around the house. Ivan came strolling around the house from the back.

"Boy, you ought to see that fire go back there; it's really something." He sat down on the ground next to Jossef.

The firemen did an exemplary job. Only a few of the trees were singed, and when the house had burned down to glowing embers between the foundation stones, they pumped water onto that, too.

Jossef had seen enough; this was not going to be a good day. He crawled, mostly on his right knee and left arm, over to the Mercedes and, screaming with the pain, pulled himself up into the seat.

"Take me to the Polaris Building," he said.

Chapter 17

We were gathered for an emergency meeting of the board in the Malamute Saloon.

Pinky and Avram dumped the boxes of money on the table and the meeting had definitely come to order.

"How much do you reckon is there?" Harry wondered.

Avram gathered up ten bundles of five thousand each and stacked them up. The stack wasn't very big. "Well, " Avram calculated, "this is fifty thousand dollars, so ten times that much is half a million. I 'd say there are several million dollars there."

"Wow." Harry went back to the bar for more scotch.

Rohrbaugh leaned across the table, scooped up an armload of bills and tossed them up in the air.

"What the hell are you doing?" Pauline demanded.

"Well, that's what they do in the movies, and I always wanted to try it. It felt pretty good." Rohrbaugh lined up behind Harry at the scotch bottle.

"The first thing we have to do is get as much as possible back to the rightful owners. Junior, give me the lists." Pauline held out her hand; I put the two lists from the Fairbanks desk into it. She spread the lists out on the table and counted.

"There's twenty businesses in Fairbanks and twenty in Anchorage, so that's a good start."

"That's funny." I was puzzled. "I counted twenty-three bars in Anchorage."

"Okay, so you count them." She pushed the Anchorage list over to me. She was right about the list, so I penciled in the last three names. I didn't point out that the Side Street was on the list and had check marks by it, and I doubted that anyone else would point it out. It seemed to me that Renaldo hadn't paid any, either, but then he had bought the bar from Gustave and Gustave had been paying, so maybe Renaldo bought the rights. Then again,

Gustave's practically giving the bar to Renaldo was almost certainly because of the protection racket, so Renaldo had already had his share. On the other hand, if Renaldo hadn't beaten up the bagman, they'd all still be paying. There were several people there smarter than me, and they weren't worried about it, so I didn't either.

"Let's start with Fairbanks," Pauline suggested. She turned to Avram, and I didn't understand why until Avram responded. He held up his fingers, but he wasn't counting on them, he was using them to make points.

"Fairbanks has been paying for nine months, so that's forty-five thousand, plus eight percent interest for nine months equals twenty-seven hundred, so they each get forty-seven thousand, seven hundred." He put his fingers away, and we started making piles of bills.

Renaldo brought wrapping paper and tape from his office, and we had a regular mailroom going. When we had twenty bundles piled up, Avram raised his fingers.

"Anchorage paid for six months so that's thirty thousand, plus eight percent interest for six months is twelve hundred dollars, so they each get thirty-one thousand, two hundred." He put his fingers away, and we started making twenty-three piles.

"Any expenses?" Pauline asked.

I piped up. "The hotel in Fairbanks cost $500 and the cars cost $50 each."

Pauline tossed me a packet of $5,000, so I put it in my pocket.

"The deductible on my car insurance was $10,000." Renaldo groused.

She tossed him two packets, then another one. "Might as well get your office repaired. Anyone else?"

"I paid for the taxi to the airport." Pinky pointed out. She tossed him a packet, then she stopped asking and just pushed a packet of five thousand to everyone else at the table. "Pain and suffering," she pronounced. "Oh, and postage." She pocketed another packet. The thing was, we still hadn't made much of a dent in the pile on the table.

"Okay, boys and girl," Pinky stood up. "Let's not get greedy here. Some of us are going to want to retire in ten or fifteen years, and I suggest we put this into a mutual fund for our old ages. Avram?"

Avram was nodding his gray mop. "With this pile, we could start our own mutual fund, but yeah, that's the way to go. I've been averaging eight percent, and that's why I suggested that for everyone."

"What's eight percent of a million bucks?" Harry wanted to know.

"Well," Avram held up his fingers, "that's only $80,000, but looks to me like there's three, four million left here. If we don't touch it for ten years, that's over another million in interest, and so on. If we divide that by . . ." He looked around the room. There were eight bar owners and me. He started over. "If we divide that by nine, we should each get $50,000 a year and never touch the principal. If we get greedy and draw a hundred thousand a year we can do that until all of us . . ." He glanced pointedly at Schneider, Renaldo, and me . . . " are way past a hundred years old." He put his fingers away.

"Vote?" Pauline asked. "I say let's do it." That seemed to settle the vote, so we piled the loose cash back into one box for Avram to invest. Each of the bar owners solemnly pocketed a reimbursement bundle, and we put the rest of the bundles into the other box for Pauline to mail.

Schneider piped up, the first words he'd uttered since we got back from Fairbanks. "Better put a phony return address on those packages, something like 'A. Friend.' What do we do if the Russians come back?"

"What I'm going to do," Pinky said, "is hire an armed guard. That will stop the one-man collections." He turned to Avram. "Tell them how many bottles of Stolichnaya were delivered today."

Avram held up his fingers. "There were only eight bottles delivered, and get this, they didn't go to Chena Ridge. Two bottles went to the penthouse at the Polaris Building, and six bottles went to room 403. Every afternoon, 2 PM like clockwork, they deliver eight bottles."

"How do you know?" I asked. Avram grinned. "Think you're the only detective, Sherlock? Remember, I have friends in all the right places."

"All well and good," Pauline decided, "but I appoint Wyatt Holmes to go back and have a look anyway, and this time no excuses because all he has to do is count Russians. That bottle counting fooled us pretty bad last time, and we don't want that happening again. Maybe someone else is delivering fifty bottles to Chena Ridge every day."

I looked around the table. Every head was nodding except mine.

R enaldo and I shared a cab, and he dropped me off at the Sheffield House. It's not that Renaldo couldn't walk. Actually, he kept himself in pretty good shape, and I suspect he did some working out, but that wasn't the point. His new Alfa was on the way, but coming by barge from Seattle. In the meantime, no one was going to see Renaldo Rodriguez walking. It wouldn't have fit his image.

It was after four in the morning when I got to the room, and Maggie wasn't there. That meant she probably wasn't coming. I was relieved to think that she'd found a new home. Maybe I missed her, but there's no need to be that honest, even with myself. Just because I could, I used three towels after my shower, and then stretched out spread-eagled right in the center of the bed. Having a king-sized bed all to yourself may be the ultimate luxury.

Thinking about *luxury* and *ultimate* got me to thinking about Connie, and I realized it was Friday morning. Maybe, just maybe, Connie would like to spend a weekend in Anchorage. Then I remembered that I'd been appointed a committee of one to go to Fairbanks, but what the heck, Connie would probably enjoy Fairbanks, too. I drifted off, determined to wake up at 7:30 and give Connie a call.

I called her at work at 2:30 Friday afternoon. She thought it was a great idea, and I even let myself think that she had missed me the past couple of weeks. I ran down to the desk and rented room 1109, which just happened to have a connecting door to 1107. You never know, Connie might want to borrow some toothpaste or something in the night.

Since I was standing at the desk anyhow, I brought my bill up to date. The Sheffield appreciates that, and maybe because of who their clientele are, they get nervous when a bill goes over a thousand dollars. I nonchalantly whipped out the packet that Pauline had tossed me and peeled off $2,200. It was nice to note that Maggie had been eating three squares a day. That made at least three hours per day that she wasn't in the bars, and when she was in the bars, it was on a full stomach, not an empty one.

The jet from Bethel landed at 8:45. I was pacing the concourse, wondering why the heck I hadn't thought to bring flowers, or candy, or maybe a diamond bracelet. There was a stir from the jetway. I saw the high heels, then the nylons, then the short skirt, and there was Connie, auburn blonde hair all fluffy and floating, eyes like a couple of sapphires, face like a Maybelline commercial, and figure from a Vargas drawing. We ran together for a hug, and I meant to tell her all that, but when I opened my mouth, I asked if she'd had dinner yet.

"Are you kidding? Eat in Bethel when I was coming to Anchorage? I'm starving."

"Any luggage?"

"Just this." That's when I noticed she was carrying an overnight case. I took the case and steered Connie's elbow outside. We slid into the first cab. It still wasn't too late to tell her that she was the most beautiful girl in the world, but the wrong words came out.

"Any particular nationality you're hankering for?" I needn't have asked. She wanted Chinese. The cab dropped us at the Pagoda at Fifth and C Street. Did I tell you that Anchorage has some of the best restaurants in the world? Put the Pagoda on your list for your next visit.

The hostess leads you into a maze of little cubicles, until you're sure that a waitress will never find you. Your cubicle will have a table that's about six inches off the floor with pillows around it for sitting. It looks like impossible gymnastics for a westerner until you sit down and find that there's a trench under the table for your feet. You're sitting in a normal manner but at floor level.

Ten seconds after you're seated, a waitress tiptoes in wearing what you're apparently supposed to think is traditional Chinese. Cute and impressive anyhow, like a long bathrobe with a little pillow attached to her belt behind. She dips right down to your level with no pops or creaks. She's offering tea or sake; I recommend both. A purist might note that the costume, the seating, and the sake are Japanese. I don't think Americans are supposed to know the difference, and if we do, we don't care.

Have the sweet and sour soup, the spareribs with pineapple, the shrimp tempura, some Kung Pao chicken, pork fried rice, and anything else; you can't go wrong. Wash it all down with piping hot sake, and know the pinnacle of human ecstasy; just don't plan on standing up right away.

I'd pictured us dancing the night away, but after that dinner, we were doing well to make it out to the cab stand. At the Sheffield, we took the elevator up to the Penthouse Lounge and squeezed ourselves into a booth, facing each other next to the big picture windows. Connie was on a sherry kick, so she ordered Harvey's Bristol Cream. I ordered Captain Morgan in Coke, and Connie brought me up to date on all of the interesting cases that the Bethel district attorney's office was handling.

City lights below us made it all kind of magic, or maybe it was the liquor. The conversation was pretty mundane, but somehow it seemed to be personal. We squeezed each other's hands during the punch lines, and pretty soon our knees were touching. My cheeks were starting to ache from three hours of constant smiling. The waitress gave us "last call" at midnight, so we had one more. By that time, we'd stopped letting our hands go between punch lines and were just holding hands, period.

When we got to our floor, I walked Connie to the door of 1109, opened the door for her and handed her the key.

Connie didn't kiss me good night. Instead, she uttered those four little words, the sweetest words in the language, the goal of every poem and love song ever written. She said; "Let's share your room."

I still had her case in my hand. I backed down the hall, opened 1107 and swept her in with a bow. Connie took her case and went into the bathroom. I slipped out, ran back to the elevators, debated running down the stairs, but decided the elevators were faster. When the elevator finally got me to the ground floor, I ran down the hall to the convenience store, grabbed a bottle of Korbel Brut out of the cooler and two wine glasses off the shelf. When Connie came out of the bathroom, I was pouring the champagne and darned near dropped the bottle.

It wasn't that I could see so much of her, it was the way what I could see was packaged. She was wearing a cloud of blue gauze that matched her eyes, what I think is called a "baby doll," and if it isn't, it should be. I handed her a glass and headed for the shower. I didn't have a silk dressing gown, so I came out wearing my pants.

Connie was propped up in the bed with the sheet pulled up to her waist and just finishing her champagne. I rushed to pour two more, opened the drapes and the sliding doors to the balcony, and turned off the lights. City lights below us made it still pretty bright in there. I sat on the other side of the bed and pulled the sheet over me while I slipped off my pants.

We toasted each other silently, tossed off the champagne, put the glasses on the nightstands, and scooted together. The door opened, the lights came on, and Maggie stumbled into the room. I buried my face in my pillow hoping for a distracting heart attack.

"Oh, hi, Connie." Maggie said. She snapped off the lights. "Shhh, don't wake Alex up, he has a terrible time getting to sleep." Maggie sat on the edge of the bed to undress. Connie had to scoot toward me, but the contact I felt was very much like a kick.

I wasn't watching. I had my face buried in the pillow, still hoping to die, but from the rustling and the shifting I gathered that Maggie had gotten naked and crawled in next to Connie.

"Oh, look, champagne . . . glug, glug, glug. This is perfect for celebrating. Do you know what we're celebrating, Connie?"

"No, Maggie, I don't know what we're celebrating." Connie's voice was dripping icicles.

"We're celebrating because I'm pregnant, isn't that wonderful?"

Connie's voice had a little less ice and a touch of incredulity. "How long have you been pregnant?" she asked.

"Two days. Oh, Connie, I got pregnant right in this bed night before last. It was the most wonderful night of my life."

"Maggie, just how long have you and Alex been sleeping together?"

"Couple of weeks, I guess. Ever since he came to town." Maggie gave a very audible yawn and the bed bounced, so I think she was stretching.

"And Alex got you pregnant?" The ice was back, big time.

"Oh no, it wasn't Alex. Alex didn't come home that night. Alex never touches me, but boy, this other guy sure did. Goodnight, Connie." Maggie started her purring snore. After that, there was an awful lot of frosty silence, but eventually Connie purred too, and I guess I went to sleep. Anyhow, I didn't die.

Chapter 18

I woke up alone in the bed. I could see a couple of towels on the floor through the open bathroom door, so Maggie had been there and it wasn't just a horrible nightmare. Then I noticed that the connecting door to 1109 was standing open. I jerked my pants on, ran over and tapped on the door. No response. I took a deep breath and peered into the room. Connie was sitting out on the balcony with her feet up on the second chair, wearing slacks, a big loose sweater, and reading a book.

She glanced up and stuck her finger in her book. "Well, it's about time. Did you promise me a trip to Fairbanks, or was that part of the awful nightmare I had last night?"

"Fairbanks coming right up. Want some breakfast first?" I was relieved that she was speaking to me; I didn't care what she said.

"No thanks, I had a lovely breakfast with Maggie an hour ago. We charged it to your room, by the way. Are you going to put some more clothes on, or have you joined a semi-nudist colony?"

I slunk into the shower. Skipping breakfast seemed like a proper penance for whatever the heck I had done wrong. Strike that. I knew perfectly well that everything I'd done was wrong, so I was just practicing my excuse in case Connie asked. She didn't.

We grabbed a cab to the airport and a Wien jet to Fairbanks. I figured I had about thirty-six hours to square things with Connie, and I didn't want to spend four of them flying the 310 back and forth. In Fairbanks, I rented a Dodge from Avis. Airport Road into town was lined with poplar trees, and here and there, stands of spruce. To Bethelites, it was like driving through a forest. The sunshine was different from Bethel or Anchorage, thinner but clearer, with a brittle feel to it. It was almost like being on a different planet, and I was already glad we'd come.

Halfway to town, we passed a mall, then a spate of fast-food restaurants, then another attempt at a mall, and we were just passing that when Connie's eyes popped wide open and her mouth dropped open, too.

"Oh-oh, oh shit, oh hell, oh damn, Alex, pull in here."

I slammed on the brakes and let the rubber howl to make the turn into the parking lot. Obviously something was terribly wrong.

"That drugstore," Connie pointed. I parked twenty feet from the door.

"Alex, see that restroom sign? I'll be waiting there. Be a sweetheart, run into the drugstore and buy a box of Tampax. The ones I want say 'super absorbency' on the package."

I might have had some questions, but Connie was already out of the car and sprinting toward the restroom. I found a box of twelve, super absorbency with flushable, biodegradable applicators. I trotted to the ladies' restroom and a hand came out to grab the box.

Ten minutes later, we were headed into town, but the mood was a bit subdued. I turned left on Noble and pulled into the courtyard parking lot at the Traveler's Inn. I carried both our bags inside; Connie had her purse in one hand and the box of Tampax in the other.

I asked the perky little girl at the desk for two rooms, but Connie said the magic words.

"Save your money, Alex, we've got the hang of sharing a room, as long as you promise there'll only be two of us. Only I hope you realize what these Tampax mean."

The desk clerk winced; obviously she knew what the Tampax meant.

"King-size or twins?" she asked.

"Twins," Connie decided.

We got a room in the middle of the horseshoe on the first floor with a view of the parking lot on the north side and a vacant lot with dumpsters on the south side, but it was only three doors from the restaurant and bar.

Connie carried the loathsome box into the bathroom and came back for her bag. She tossed that on the bed by the south windows, so I tossed my bag on the bed by the door. There were only four feet separating the beds, but they had the feeling of the Grand Canyon.

"Want some lunch?" I asked. She shook her head. "I don't suppose you want to drive up to Circle Hot Springs and bask in the mineral pools?" I asked.

"You got that right. Alex, I'm really sorry, but what I want right now is a nap. I didn't get much sleep last night with Maggie snoring in one ear and you snoring in the other. Why don't you be a good boy and do up Fairbanks by yourself? Just don't bring home any strays, and I promise that by this evening I'll be ready to eat and drink you under the table." She had kicked off her shoes, so she stood on tiptoe to give me a wonderful promissory kiss, full of Crest and Revlon, and what I took to be genuine regret. She gave me a hug so I wouldn't forget she had breasts, and then sort of steered me toward the door. I took the hint.

I walked along the sidewalk past the parked cars and the next three rooms to the coffee shop and had a patty melt to make up for missing breakfast. I have to admit that I dawdled over three extra cups of coffee while I built up my nerve to go up to Chena Ridge.

Days and nights had been a little crazy, so I may have lost count, though I think it had only been four days since my last trip up the ridge road. The trees were already losing their springtime yellow-green for their darker summer color.

Fairbanks does that. Seasons move fast, and I guess they have to, to get them all in. In most of America, spring days get longer by about two and a half minutes a day, but in Fairbanks, where they come out of December with three hours of daylight and finish June with twenty-three, they gain about six and a half minutes a day. If it had been four days since the last trip, that's already a half hour more daylight.

I skipped the turnout where we had parked before and found another half a mile farther up the road. Instead of walking back on the road, I walked down into the woods until I felt hidden. The birch trees still had the early spring smell, like pitch and promise, with no dust on the leaves yet. Sunlight was filtered to a yellow green, like the polarized light you see with shooter's glasses; not a happy association. There is nothing like expecting to be shot from any direction at any moment to keep you focused.

The hill was pretty steep, with the road on top and the river at the bottom. Once in a while I could hear a splash from the river, probably salmon jumping, and it seemed like I could sense the power and movement down there. They say that horses can smell water. I don't think humans are supposed to have that ability, but I could smell the river. It smelled like wet dirt and fish, with a hint of moldy leaves to it. There also seemed to be another smell in the air, but I couldn't quite identify it.

There's a special feel to the woods when there are just you and the birds. You might be able to get among trees just as thick in Central Park, and see nothing but trees when you looked around, but the feeling is different. You know how you can feel a presence when someone else is in a room with you? Maybe the flip side of that is being able to feel when you're the only human presence in a good bit of real estate, unless that all-alone feeling is what you get when fifty rifles are pointed at you.

There wasn't any sound coming from the direction of the house, and the birds seemed to be happy, but I took my time and kept quiet anyhow. For one thing, I didn't have my .357 with me because we came by jet with only hand carry, so it was back at the hotel in Anchorage. Thing is, it wouldn't have mattered much. If there were fifty soldiers in that house, and they all decided to shoot me, I might have taken out six of them with the .357. Being shot by only forty-four Kalashnikovs instead of fifty didn't seem all that great a distinction.

I was picking up the smell of a backyard barbecue, but none of the clamor. When I got closer, the odor was pretty strong, like maybe they let the barbecue burn while they spread out through the woods to blast an intruder. I wasn't quite crawling through the woods, but I was doing a lot of tree impersonating.

I was so busy looking for snipers that I nearly tripped over the berm around the parking lot. I hadn't realized I was there because I hadn't seen any roof, and when I peeked over the berm, there also weren't any walls. The foundation not only smelled but looked like a barbecue pit that had been packed full of charcoal. I stood up and walked back to the car. The missing house explained why there were no deliveries to Chena Ridge, but it didn't preclude fifty soldiers who might be somewhere else. The next step seemed to be checking on Avram's information about the Polaris Building.

The Polaris Building has a coffee shop, a liquor store, a bar, and offices on the main floor; the rest is all apartments. There's a little alcove by the elevators with a couple of chairs and an artificial tree with flowers that look like gardenias but smell like dust. I made myself at home and waited for the 2 PM delivery that Avram had promised. A kid with two packages showed up right on schedule. I didn't accost him, but I did manage to stand between him and the elevator buttons.

"Those packages for 403 and the penthouse?" I asked.

He didn't answer me, but he squirmed his affirmative. He had the two boxes in his arms and one hand sticking out to punch the button. I put a $20 bill between his extended fingers.

"I'll take those up for you," I offered.

"I don't think I should do that." He was shaking the twenty at me, wanting me to take it back, but also not wanting to drop the boxes.

I whipped out my detective badge and let him get a glimpse of it. "Oh yes, you definitely should do that. The only question is, do you take the twenty, or this?" I flashed the badge again. He had a caving-in expression, so I dropped the badge back in my pocket and took the boxes.

"You'll be sorry," he said. "They never tip." He was backing up, and when he hit the tree, he turned around and fled. I already had the elevator opening.

I hope you noticed, I didn't say anything about police, or arrest. That would be strictly illegal, and as I said before, impersonating an officer is a felony. I just offered to give him the badge or the twenty and he opted for the twenty.

The guy who opened the door at 403 was a caricature, made of 2x2s and wearing a mask from *The Night of the Living Dead*. He fit the door lengthwise, but I could see past him on both sides, and there sure weren't fifty soldiers in there. In fact, the only sign of habitation that I could see was a couple of pizza boxes on the floor. The odor that wafted out was half pizza, half dirty socks. He grabbed the larger box and slammed the door. The kid was right: no tip.

It took a while to get an answer at the penthouse, but I could hear bumping and scraping inside. An eye appeared at the peephole, and the door finally swung open. The guy standing, or rather leaning, there had a cast on his left leg and a cast in a sling on his right arm. He was wrestling a crutch and trying to hold the door with his left hand. He jerked his head for me to come in, so I carried the package into the room and plunked it on a dining table.

"Open it." That wasn't a request, it was a command, but I could see that he'd have a problem with only one hand, so I tore off the paper and unscrewed the cap on one of the bottles.

"Now get out," he said. He was an ordinary-looking guy, about my size, and no outstanding features, except that he had the meanest, most evil eyes that I had seen on a human being since I left 403. There was something familiar about him, but I couldn't place it. I was sure I'd never seen him before, but that sense of familiarity was nagging at me. I backed toward the door. He had an ugly .45 automatic stuck in his belt, and his left hand was hovering, so that was distracting. I was walking backward but sneaking quick peeks over my shoulder, not wanting to take my eyes off the automatic but also not wanting to trip over anything.

I opened the door and stepped out, feeling lucky to be alive and in the hallway. It wasn't until the elevator started down that I realized what was familiar. The guy had been wearing pants and a shirt exactly like the new ones I had bought in Anchorage.

Chapter 19

Jossef had gone through his pockets during the painful ride into town from Chena Ridge, and had come up with $4,283.27. That had got him into the Polaris, but that was about the end of it. He needed to get back into business fast. He sensed that there was some flaw in the insurance business, and he was going to have to work on that. The sex trades seemed to be pretty well covered in Fairbanks, supply already way ahead of demand, and no unfulfilled niches that he could think of.

He considered getting back into drugs, maybe hooking up with one of Samson's old contacts in Columbia, but as some wise capo once said, "it takes money to make money," and Jossef didn't have any. Then he remembered that he owned a massage parlor out on South Cushman Street.

With a firm grip of will over pain, he hobbled out to the elevator and punched "lobby." The Mercedes was parked at an expired meter. He managed to get into it and discovered that he could drive it. By reaching with his left hand to put the car in Drive, all he needed was his right foot, and he had that. He wheeled into the lot at the massage parlor and parked sideways across three spaces with the bumper next to the stairs.

He made it, step, clunk, scrape, step, clunk, scrape, into the office. Carla proudly showed him the books. She had changed the leather outfit for black rubber, stretched so tight that it was see-through around every muscle, and her gumdrop nipples appeared about to pop through.

Carla's books consisted of a loose-leaf notebook with chronological entries:

Mr. Smith $180.00
Mr. Smith $240.00
Mr. Smith $60.00
Mr. Smith .... $500.00 (around the world)
Mr. Smith .... $20.00 (just a shower)
Mr. Smith.................$180.00

On and on the Smith action went. All in all, business had been good. After expenses, half of the fees went to the operators, half accrued to Jossef, and he was pleasantly surprised to find that his share for the month was $9,640. He realized that the reason he'd always thought of the business as peanuts was that the business had been paying protection money all these months. Now, if he didn't pay $5,000 to the protection racket, the $9,000 was his to keep.

He supposed that Carla was skimming twenty percent and he considered blowing her away, which would make his take even more. Then he considered spending his days at the parlor and dealing with the steam and the women in their underwear, and decided to keep Carla for a while.

Carla squeaked her rubber skirt into the office and tossed the mail onto the desk. Most of it was ads for adult toys and videos, plus a couple of utility bills. Jossef tossed the pile into the wastebasket and checked out the package in the plain brown wrapper. It was from *A. Friend*, postmarked in Anchorage, with the notation, "Insurance Rebate."

Jossef was way too savvy for that trick. He checked that it wasn't ticking, but mail bombs never have timers. Even if you estimate when a package should arrive, and double the time, it will still go off in a post office somewhere. It was undoubtedly going to explode when he tore the tape or removed the wrapper. He wedged the package between the cast and his chest so that the sling held it up and hobbled into the janitor's closet.

A big steel bucket with wringer and mop was sitting in the sink. He pulled the mop out of the bucket, carefully set the package into the bucket, and ran the faucet to cover the package with several inches of water. He could toss it into a dumpster after it soaked a while.

Carla's bank was half a Tampax carton piled with loose bills; apparently she bought Tampax by the case. Jossef stuffed $9,500 into his pockets and left the $140 for seed money. The money in his pockets felt pretty good. It was mostly tens and twenties, instead of the hundreds he was used to, but it sure beat having his pockets empty.

He stepped, bumped, and scraped his way back to the parking lot and started to hobble to the Mercedes. He remembered that he had forgotten to mention to Carla that the janitor shouldn't open the package, and wondered if it was worth going all the way back inside, but he noticed a uniformed, armed guard leaning against the wall in front of the Squadron Club taxi-dancing emporium next door.

Obviously something was up, and he wondered if it was something he should know about, so he hobbled across the lot and into the Squadron Club. The guard looked him over, eyes almost hidden by the brim of his cap, but continued to lean against the wall, sucking on a toothpick.

The club was dark, not the sort of place that has windows. A jukebox was wailing a slow dance. A dozen taxi dancers sat in the folding chairs along the wall wearing shorts or miniskirts and halters. Some were reading magazines, a couple were filing away at false fingernails, and the rest were just staring into space, or rather at the empty dance floor. Two working stiffs were perched on bar stools nursing beers but didn't appear likely to be buying tickets for two-dollar dances any time soon.

The bar was sixty feet long with the two drinkers spread twenty feet apart. Jossef clumped over to the near end of the bar and climbed onto a stool. Bambi, the owner, came right over with a shot glass of vodka and leaned against her side of the bar. She was wearing skin-tight hot pants and an indecisive garment that was either a halter or a bra. There wasn't much in it, so it didn't much matter. Her hair was bobbed at her earlobes and bleached platinum blonde, but it took on the reds and greens of the lighted beer signs. Jossef put the standard price, two five-dollar bills, on the bar. As a professional courtesy to her next-door neighbor, Bambi picked up only one of the bills.

"I hear you were in some kind of accident," Bambi said, not terribly perceptively considering the casts.

"Yeah, I was trying to rescue a friend from a burning building, falling timbers and so on, just a few broken bones. How come the armed guard outside?"

"Oh, haven't you heard?" Bambi gave up on getting gossip and decided to give some, leaning farther across the bar to imply confidentiality. "All the bars are hiring guards. Didn't you get your insurance rebate from A. Friend?"

Jossef choked on his vodka. Bambi reached across the bar to pound him on the back, which caused his arm cast to swing in the sling and pound him on the front. He got his coughing fit under control and used a damp bar towel to wipe his mouth.

Bambi leaned farther across the bar, her top drooping down to display nipples, and lowered her voice to keep this confidential among business owners. "You'll probably get yours. The package has all of our back payments in it plus interest, and a note." She looked both ways to be sure no one was listening, although the nearest customer was twenty feet down the bar and intent on picking his nose.

"The note says that the Russian Mafia is all a bluff. It's just that Ed Asner guy operating all by himself. Everyone hired a guard, and the next time he shows his face, we'll blow him away."

She lowered her voice to a whisper; "We got his picture off an advertisement for a TV show. Do you think we could get in trouble for that?"

Jossef's coughing fit came back. He slid off the stool, barely escaping Bambi's roundhouse whack, and hobbled rapidly out the door.

When he held up the package, blue water streamed out for a while. He ripped off the soggy paper and out tumbled bundles of hundred-dollar bills. Ink had run on the note, so it was practically blank. Blue ink was staining the wrapper and the first couple of bundles of bills. When he tried to wring out a bundle of money, his fingers turned blue.

He started at the back corner of the room, climbing down his crutch to kneel on the floor. He peeled the wet bills loose, one at a time, and papered the floor, the desk, the chair, and back to the floor, with a single layer of drying bills. He papered his way right to the door, stuck the last couple of wet bundles in a pocket, locked the door to the office, and headed home to tell Yuri the bad news.

"So, you see, Yuri, with twenty guys in Fairbanks and another twenty in Anchorage, all hired to shoot you on sight, maybe you should get out of town for a while."

Yuri didn't appear inclined to argue, so Jossef continued.

"It has been good working with you, although I suppose you do realize that all of this is your fault. If you had just continued making the collections like you were supposed to, none of this would have happened." Jossef felt his anger rising and reached for his gun to shoot Yuri's ears off, but he didn't want to make that much noise in his penthouse suite. Instead, he pulled out one of the soggy bundles of bills.

"Here's something for old time's sake, and to speed you on your journey." Jossef peeled off seven of the wet bills, hesitated over the eighth, waffled over the ninth, but then in a sudden fit of generosity, gave Yuri ten of the wet hundreds.

"It's probably best if you get out of town right away before someone sees you here." Jossef leaned his crutch against the desk and extended his good arm to Yuri for a hug. Yuri dutifully stepped into the embrace, and Jossef hugged him so long and hard that Yuri was afraid Jossef would notice the hundred thousand dollars that was sewn into Yuri's jacket. Finally, Jossef released Yuri and sort of turned him toward the door with a gentle push. Yuri bolted.

Jossef sat down behind the desk to consider whether he should invest his new capital in cocaine or just import a small bale of pot. He was still undecided when the phone rang.

"Hello, Jossef, Seidel here. Just a friendly reminder, haven't you forgotten something?"

Seidel's phony cheerful tone stood the hairs up on Jossef's neck. "Not that I know of, what are you talking about?"

"Well, heh, heh, heh, our deal was $5,000 per week for as long as you kept my soldiers, and three of them haven't come back yet. Right now, you only owe me $30,000 but what the heck, why don't we just pay by the month? Since we're friends, let's just round it down and call it $50,000 per month. That keeps the math simple, heh, heh, heh."

"Hey, I don't have your soldiers. They interfered with a flight crew, so they're doing three-to-five in a federal ice house."

"Well, Jossef, it's none of my business what you've done with them. My only concern is that they're not back yet."

"Look, that wasn't my fault. I asked for soldiers, you rented me Neanderthals, they didn't do me any good, so really, you owe me a refund."

"Jossef, there are no bad soldiers, only bad capos. They were not in jail when I rented them to you. If you let them get into jail, that is your lookout. We said $5,000 per week each until they were returned. I'm trying to give you a break here. Would it be easier for you to just send the money to the address I gave you, or would it be helpful if I send a few people up there to collect?"

Jossef looked out across the wooded hills beyond Fairbanks, and suddenly they seemed cluttered and stifling. He remembered the neat brown desert hills around the kibbutz in Israel. He caught a vision of his future life, a future in which Ivan and Boris dealt with Carla and mailed $5,000 per month to Jossef, while he himself relaxed and hoed lettuce on the lush green irrigated fields of the kibbutz without a worry in the world. He wouldn't have the easy retirement his father had, because he didn't have diamonds to spread around, but if Boris and Ivan actually sent the money, he could live very well.

But first, there was one detail he had to attend to. There is more than one way to skin an Italian.

"Seidel, you are a cheap, chiseling scumbag. You're a disgrace to our profession and a blot on the reputation of Mother Russia. Obviously you're the result of your mother's coupling with a donkey. You may be a big man down there in little Washington state, but bucko, this is Alaska. This is my territory, and if you and your little friends think you can muscle in here, you're welcome to try it. You bring all of your worthless soldiers you want, and I'll give you a lesson in how a real capo runs his territory. Just come on up any old time. I'll be at my headquarters in the Malamute Saloon in Anchorage." Jossef hung up the phone and bump, scraped into the bedroom to start packing. He tried whistling Havah Nagila, but couldn't remember the tune.

Chapter 20

*C*onnie was propped up on pillows, sitting on her bed but wearing skirt and blouse, nylons and pumps. She gave me a brilliant smile and laid her book, open, spine up, on the comforter beside her.

"Have a fun day?" she asked.

"Lonesome and dull," I assured her. "Furthermore, I'm starving; want to do something about that?"

"Starved for food, or affection?"

"Both."

She spread her arms in welcome and I started for the bed, but by the time I got to her she was already standing up. She gave me the hug and kiss and suddenly I forgot all about food, but she hadn't.

"Let's go find you something to eat." She reached for her jacket.

I turned left, away from town, and left again on Gaffney Road. The Broiler is at the edge of the demilitarized zone. If you don't turn off there, you'll be going through the main gates of Fort Wainwright, but if you're hungry, you are going to turn off there. The hostess met us at the door, led us past the gleaming dark chromium cavern of bar on the left and into the brightly lit dining room. I think it's called *homey*, if that's a synonym for small, but there's nothing small about the food.

We ordered the African lobster tails, of course, which is the reason for going to The Broiler, and reason enough to go to Fairbanks for that matter. I know half a dozen places in the world that do lobsters exactly right, and they start with The Broiler. A bottle of 1963 Chenin Blanc is the perfect lubricant, and we spent an hour perched on the pinnacle of civilization. Connie was beaming, but we weren't chatting. It's the sort of meal where you close your eyes to savor each bite, and replace it as soon as it's gone.

At five minutes to eight, we scooted kitty-corner across the street to the Wagon Wheel Club. It's a long, low wooden building that evokes the Old

West, and of course is decorated with wheels and wagon parts. We stepped through the door to utter silence, and a waitress hustled us to a table in the center of the room next to a volleyball-court-sized dance floor. The room was full, about fifty couples, all of them watching one table that was set up next to the organ.

On Saturday nights, KFAR radio did a one-hour broadcast from the Wagon Wheel Club, and it was about one minute to airtime. An announcer, inexplicably called "talent" in the broadcast business, was wearing a sport coat and tie and reading through papers he had on a clipboard. The other guy at the table, inexplicably called the "engineer" in broadcast circles, was wearing a plaid shirt and jeans and was obviously too young to be in a bar. He had built a dike on his half of the table with amplifier, telephone, radio, and a home-made chassis featuring a repeat coil stolen from the phone company, all in the service of sending the broadcast down the phone lines to the station.

The engineer was listening intently to earphones from the radio and hold-ing one finger aloft like Leonard Bernstein about to give the downbeat to the New York Symphony. The finger sliced the air like Zorro's sword, and Swede Hahn cut loose with ten thousand watts of organ. The theme song, of course, was "Wagon Wheels," and if you don't know that song, you can be sure that your parents do. It's been around for about a hundred years, but it was written especially for Swede Hahn to render on that organ.

"Wagon wheels, wagon wheels, keep on a turnin', wagon wheels. Roll along, sing your song, wagon wheels, carry me ho-oo-ome . . ." The song evokes end-less prairies, loneliness, courage, and determination, which are appropriate to Fairbanks. When it's played on a high-powered organ with unlimited, floor-shaking bass, treble in the stratosphere, and all of that in a closed room, you become part of the resonating chamber.

Waitresses did manage to circulate, and we did manage to plow into some serious Captain Morgan. Connie had abandoned her sherry kick and joined me in the elixir of life, so it was an all-stops-out hour, so to speak. Once in a while Swede would pause, and the talent would hunch over his table microphone, one hand holding a paper, the other plugging one ear with a finger, and read like crazy for thirty seconds before Swede blasted us back into the organ.

When your entire being is wrapped up in music, it's hard to count drinks, and we didn't. I know the broadcast ended, and I know Swede continued to play and people danced, including us, I think. Sometime in the night Swede quit, and I have an elusive memory of a parking lot and another bar, but the next thing I really know is that I woke up crosswise of the bed with my clothes on, and Connie right beside me doing a soft little breathing act with fumes that you would not want to get close to with a match.

We spent about forty-five minutes on damage control, quiet but companionable, taking turns in the bathroom, and held hands on the way to the restaurant. The Bloody Marys were lifesavers, made of V-8 instead of tomato juice, and with plenty of Tabasco. The celery hearts were crisp, but tender, perfect for acclimating our stomachs to accept solid food.

You have to depend on and believe the clocks in Fairbanks because the sun never gets very high. Mostly it just goes around, so it's south at noon, and as high as it's going to get, but it's only a little lower, and north in the middle of the night. It ducks down behind the peaks around Eagle Summit for an hour or so at midnight, but it isn't much of an instrument for telling time. The clock in the restaurant said 2:30, which I took to be afternoon and an hour and a half past checkout time.

Connie had used enough of the little cylinders that the residue fit in her purse, so she abandoned the box in the room. We called a cab and cruised out Gaffney Road, looking for the car. It wasn't at The Broiler or the Wagon Wheel, so we went back to Cushman Street and headed south. The car was parked in front of the Carousel, doors open, lights on, engine running, and very nearly out of gas. We made the transfer, and I tipped the cabby a five. He didn't seem to notice anything unusual about our search.

We grabbed a Wien jet back to Anchorage at 4:30. That would get us there just in time for Connie to check in for the evening Bethel flight.

A guy ahead of us in line caught my attention, mostly because he was wearing a very large, very black beard, and a mustache to match. The hair sticking out under his felt hat was lighter with a touch of gray threatening it. His clothes were a little strange, but nothing I could put my finger on, except that he wore a kind of quilted jacket buttoned tight while the rest of us wore light jackets hanging open. I wondered if he was into some orthodox religion with a Samson complex, because he had a lot more beard even than sourdoughs usually wear. I guessed that he was in some Jewish sect, but then I always think people with oversized beards are Jewish.

Mt. Denali was clear, and the pilot detoured to give us the view, so we were going to have to hustle when we landed.

We were scooting down the concourse in Anchorage, the guy with the beard scurrying along ahead of us, when we were blocked by a solid stream of passengers coming off a Seattle flight. We bunched up and waited; there wasn't any choice if you were headed for the next gate. Suddenly the bearded guy jumped as if he'd been goosed with a cattle prod and bolted toward an exit. He charged through a revolving door, way too fast for the door. There was a flurry at the exit and when the door came around again the beard was stuck in it, and there was Ed Asner, eyes like saucers peering through the door, mouth wide open, exactly like a guppy in a fishbowl.

I didn't watch to see if he got his beard back because I was a lot more interested in what had startled him, and I didn't get it at first. There was just a steady stream of working-type stiffs coming out, but then I began to see a kind of homogeneity about them. They were together, no women, no children, no suits mixed in, and they all had the same vacant-but-menacing expressions.

I guessed about fifty of them went by in a solid line before a break came and we ducked through. I stopped Connie at her gate, gave her a peck on the cheek, and handed over her case. She looked perplexed, but I didn't have time to explain.

"Thanks, Connie. It was a super great weekend and I'll see you in Bethel soon." I ran down the concourse following the homogeneous parade.

Chapter 21

I was on the escalator, ten people behind what I was starting to think of as the army. They gathered around a carousel; it gave a lurch, red light flashing, and luggage came around the bend. The first luggage off was golf clubs, zipped into traveling bags so you couldn't see the clubs. The army started picking them up, ignoring the rest of the passengers who were instinctively cowering in the background to wait.

People do play golf in Anchorage. In fact, I think the course at Russian Jack Springs is sort of famous as being the roughest, most primitive course in the world. Some idiots even use red balls and play in the wintertime, but these guys did not look like a pro golf tour on the road.

I bulled my way to the Avis desk, and fortunately, Trisha was on duty so I didn't have to show my badge. I tossed her my driver's license and a credit card, said "Any car, quick," and grabbed her telephone. I dialed the Malamute, the waitress who answered said, "Okey doky," and Renaldo came on the line.

"Renaldo, there's a bomb planted in the club, set to go off in half an hour. Get the people out. There's probably a bomb in all the other clubs too, so warn your neighbors." I hung up. Trisha's eyes had gone double sized. She handed me a key and I ran for the lot across the street. The soldiers were queuing into a Roberts Tours bus at the curb.

I made record time to the alley behind the Malamute and parked next to the exit door. A pickup truck was there ahead of me, and I'd just started to run past that when the door opened and Greg the bandleader came out carrying armfuls of amplifiers. I skidded to a halt and charged the backdoor.

"Hey, man, don't go in there, there's a bomb about to go off." He was shouldering me out of his way to go back in.

"Yeah, I heard," I told him.

Greg ran to the bandstand, grabbed a six-foot-tall speaker set under each arm and ran back toward his pickup. I sprinted through the bar to the front door, loosened the setscrew with my pocketknife, and took the knob off the inside. I could see a solid line of people milling around on the other side of Fourth Avenue, some still with drinks in their hands, waiting for the show. One setscrew holds the inside knob on. Loosen the screw, pull the knob off, and there's just a square shaft left that operates the mechanism. I jerked the door open, reached around and pulled the outside knob off, square shaft and all, and dropped them in my pocket. With no knob, no one was going to open the door.

I ran back to Renaldo's office and started making phone calls. I dialed 911 and screamed that there was a bomb in the Malamute Saloon, hung up and dialed the State Troopers. "There's a hostage situation at the Malamute Saloon, thirty people being held by a gang of terrorists." I hung up and dialed the Alaska National Guard.

"This is Governor Miller's office. There's a race riot on Fourth Avenue, *gussaks* killing Eskimos at the Malamute Saloon, get down there." That was an inspired message because the Alaska National Guard is ninety-eight percent Native, and they've been expecting that call for fifty years. I dialed the MPs at Elmendorf, shouting that fifty airmen were running naked down Fourth Avenue.

I rifled the desk. The .44 revolver that Renaldo had confiscated was in the drawer. It had a nasty nick in the barrel, but it wasn't bent. I spun the cylinder; it seemed to work. Renaldo had a little clock radio on the desk. I turned that up loud, left the light on, and locked the brand-new office door behind me. That would give the Russians something to focus on for a while. The Roberts Tour bus was pulling up out front and I could hear sirens in the distance. Greg seemed to have made his final trip; there was nothing on the bandstand but a broken stool. I ran to the front door and used the knob with shaft from my pocket to open it.

Men were spilling out of the bus onto the sidewalk, carrying rifles and looking around. I used the .44 to guide them to the proper door. I shot the no parking sign, which made a terrible clang, then blew the big front mirror off the bus, which showered glass on the exiters. I shot out a couple of bus windows, mostly so that everyone could see me standing in the doorway. The bus lurched forward, stopped again with a screech, and bodies piled out double time.

I left the front door swinging open, but took the shaft with me, and ran through the bar and out the back door. I jammed the rental car tight against the back door so that it wouldn't open and ran down the alley just in time to see a dozen police cars circling like a wagon train to block off Fourth Avenue. I stayed outside the circle and joined the spectators across the street. The crowds seemed to be growing in spite of the cops, who were waving guns and threatening to shoot us if we didn't leave.

Pinky was working the crowd. He had two ice buckets and was selling beer.

The bus was gone, the Russians were inside, and the front door of the Malamute had swung shut. I was hoping that would happen, and the door was going to stay shut because I had the knobs in my pocket. I took them out and tossed them down the hill into the parking lot below.

A big black van screeched up Fourth from the direction of C Street and parked next to the cop cars. A dozen men in black pajamas and riot masks came pouring out, cradling rifles and looking exactly like a SWAT team from the movies. A silver van lurched up from the other way and men in space suits came busting through the police lines, looking for the bombs.

The SWAT team hunkered down behind police cars and trained rifles on the Malamute. Someone on a bullhorn began demanding the release of the hostages. Three National Guard halftracks ripped around the corner off E Street, way too fast to stop when they saw the cop cars. They blasted right through the line, hubcaps and fenders flying. The crowd cheered, the halftracks slid to a stop in front of the Malamute, and suddenly there were uniformed guards standing up manning machine guns.

The SWAT team moved up to lean across the halftracks. There were two or three bullhorns now, demanding this and that, and enough firepower aimed at the Malamute for WW III, but everyone was practicing restraint. The heck with that. I whipped out the .44 and fired my last shot through the plate-glass window. A volley of automatic fire came out, pinging off the halftracks and whining away over the crowd. The plate glass was no more. The troops outside all fired at once, and the war was on. People were diving off the sidewalk, sliding down toward the parking lot on Third. I saw Renaldo in the crowd and worked my way over to grab him, shoving several hesitant jumpers off the edge in the process.

We ducked and ran up the sidewalk past E Street. After we crossed E, things were calmer, just a few latecomers running down Fourth to see what the racket was. By the time we crossed F, it sounded more like Fourth of July than an afternoon on the Golan Heights, and when we rounded the corner onto G, all we could hear were the occasional hand grenades and the chatter of the machine guns.

We had the coffee shop at the Sheffield all to ourselves. Renaldo ordered the breaded prawns; I ordered a chicken-fried steak.

"You know, Alex, I've been thinking."

I couldn't help cringing. That statement has been the prelude to an awful lot of problems.

Renaldo daubed his mustache with his napkin, just in case there was tartar sauce on it, but of course, there wasn't. "I don't think the bar business is really for me." He daubed his lips and took a sip of his coffee. I waited. He was going to drop another shoe, possibly right on my head.

"I got a couple of phone calls while you were goofing off in Fairbanks. One was from Gustave. He says that if the Russians are really gone, he'd like to buy his bar back, and he's planning to remodel, so the fact that you've reduced it to a hole in the ground won't stop him."

I waited. He had said, "two phone calls." The steak was pretty good. I do love that thick brown gravy they use.

Renaldo held a prawn by the tail and pulled the last morsel out with his teeth, then—of course—he daubed his mustache.

"The other phone call was from a guy I met in Panama when I was setting up those water-ski tours."

I remembered the tour idea, "Ski from Ocean to Ocean," and it might have worked if the lock operators had been more cooperative.

Renaldo continued. "This old friend is involved with a gold mine in Venezuela and they're offering me a partnership just to handle the bookkeeping and shipping. He says his share is running thirty thousand a week, and they could double that if they had a good comptroller on board." He attacked another shrimp.

"And you're seriously considering the offer?" I asked.

"Yeah, I'm pretty serious about it. I bought a ticket to Venezuela this afternoon."

The door opened behind me and Maggie walked in, carrying a little suitcase. She slid onto the bench beside me and set her case on the floor.

"Hi, Maggie. This is my college roommate, Renaldo. Renaldo, Maggie is my *eelook* from Bethel."

They reached across the table for a formal handshake.

"Just what the heck is an *eelook*?" Renaldo wanted to know.

Maggie and I both laughed. "An *eelook* is a buddy, a friend, a sidekick, a partner. Get your mind out of the gutter." It suddenly struck me that Maggie was sober and I made the obvious remark: "Maggie, you're sober."

"Yep," she said, "I quit drinking yesterday. I'm pregnant, so no more. Alex, do you know Willie? He's Mary Peterson's boy from Grayling? He has a job at Swanson's store and a house by the river. He wants to marry me, so you can take me back to Bethel now."

"Maggie," I said, "that's really wonderful. We'll take off for Bethel just as soon as I check out of the hotel. In the meantime, have some supper. We can charge it to the room."

An Excerpt from the Upcoming Book

Yukon Murders

By Don Porter

Chapter 1: First Visit

7:00 Monday morning
Alakanuk, Alaska

Two men stood in a pool of yellow light from the single bulb hanging above the cash register. Demientoff, tall, stocky, was dressed for inside work in plaid shirt and jeans. His visitor was shorter, slight, still wearing his beaver parka, now unzipped and hanging open to reveal a blue wool shirt. His matching beaver hat was pushed back on his head; wolf mitts dangled from a lanyard around his neck. The rest of the store remained dark and eerily quiet, shadows swaying as the light bulb swung tiny ovals. Demientoff was making a show of moving stacks of bills from the safe to the register, counting each stack. He seemed to be taking a perverse satisfaction in keeping his visitor waiting.

The visitor stood quietly, leaning casually against the counter. He appeared to be subserviently patient, but his mind was churning.

Keep smiling. Mustn't show that bastard how much I hate him. Pompous ass. He thinks I'm here to talk about the sharing.

He did it again this morning, his superior, "Oh, Hello, Shorty," as though I was some bum seeking favors. Without me, he'd be the bum, probably scrabbling for a subsistence lifestyle and looking for satisfaction in a whiskey bottle. I gave him this store as a gift, set him up for life, and he never even thanked me. He should be treating me with respect.

Demientoff had started with the twenties, was down to counting out twenty ones, taking his time, turning each bill face up, Washington gazing to the left. The visitor pushed himself away from the counter, pointed at the glass gun case. "Hey, Demientoff, I need a new .30-06. Let me check one out while you're busy."

"That old blunderbuss of yours finally give up? Remington or Winchester?"

"Bolt action, don't need a scope."

Demientoff stopped counting, shrugged his irritation, but turned to open the locked case with a key on his ring and handed a rifle to the visitor.

"Try this one." He went back to counting money.

"Not bad." The visitor slid the bolt, dry fired it. He aimed at a shadow at the end of the aisle, dry fired it again. "Nice balance. How about a special price for an old friend?"

"No can do. Price barely covers expenses."

There it was again. Haughty sneer. He had not only forgotten that I'm his benefactor, but wasn't even acknowledging me as a friend.

The visitor slipped a cartridge into the chamber. A snowmachine coughed to life outside; the driver revved his engine.

Demientoff looked up in shock at the rifle pointed his way. "Hey, be careful where you're pointing that thing."

"I am, very careful." The visitor shot him between the eyes. Demientoff flew back against the wall, brains and blood spattering on the rough boards. He crumpled to the floor, blood spurting and pooling around him. The visitor stepped over the body to reach the polishing rag and the little bottle of gun oil.

He doesn't look so high and mighty now. Still too good for me, Demientoff?

The visitor ejected the shell, pocketed it, poured a few drops of oil down the barrel and wiped the gun clean with the polishing rag. He carefully set the rifle back in its slot in the rack, made sure there was no sign of its having been moved. The key ring still dangled from the lock. He locked the case and bent to stuff the ring into Demientoff's pocket.

You have to plan, think of all the details. Stay calm, don't hurry, don't make mistakes. That's my special genius. I never make mistakes.

He took the bills out of the register to make the killing appear to be a robbery, being careful not to touch anything but the money. He used his handkerchief to open the back door, letting the lock snap to behind him. At seven-fifteen it was still dark, but a few people were moving in the village, blocked from his view by the silhouette of the store. He could hear snow machines running, dogs barking for feeding, somewhere a door slamming. Alakanuk River below him was ghostly white, his snowmachine an indistinct black shadow parked on the trail.

A ridge of unmarked snow covered the edge of the loading dock. He jumped over that, landed a foot short of the hard-packed trail, and sank inches deep into soft snow on the river ice. All part of his plan; he wanted to leave tracks in the snow.

Just one more detail, the elegant solution.

He pulled the wolf-fur cap out of his parka and tossed it up toward the edge of the loading dock.

It's not my fault that big gussak got in my way. I'll smash him if necessary. That's what sets me apart from the losers. Nothing stops me. The gussak struts around the village like he owns it. Maybe a few years in jail will put him in his place.

A hundred yards downstream an engine revved; the headlight of a machine flashed on snow and bumped down onto the river. The visitor started the Arctic Cat and drove up the trail toward the Yukon. He was careful not to drive too fast; he mustn't appear to be running away. Just fast enough to keep out of the light from the machine behind.

10:00 Monday morning
Bethel, Alaska

Getting a call at ten on a Monday morning in December sent a groan around the room. It meant someone had to fly. None of us was particularly eager, but that is why we were there. Vickie took the call, wrote an entry on the blank schedule sheet, and pointed at me. She pantomimed a pistol, shooting me with her extended finger and a click of her tongue.

"Trooper Tim needs a ride to Alakanuk in an hour. Expect four or five hours standby. Just two seats, the third passenger will be in a body bag." She went back to reading her book, propping her elbow on her blotter, cupping delicate chin in hand. Her ruby nails disappeared under a honey-blonde wave that swung forward to mask her face, making a personal privacy curtain.

Vickie, presiding over the bare wooden waiting room at Bushmaster Air Service, was an anomaly, but a welcome one, like finding a lush tropical island in the middle of the North Atlantic. In a fuzzy blue sweater, gray skirt, heels and hose, she seemed to be trying to raise the tone of our operation all by herself.

The pilots who were reading magazines or napping around the room were the scruffy lot you would expect in bush Alaska, dressed for winter, but with zippers open down the fronts and up the legs of their snowsuits. I marked my place in the Donald Westlake book I was reading. I feel a kinship with his Dortmunder character. It seems like the harder I work on a plan, the less likely it is to succeed. I stood up and zipped, pulled a parka on over my snowsuit, grabbed a beaver fur cap and a pair of wolf mitts from the chair arm, picked up my flight bag, and went out to prepare for Trooper Tim.

When I opened the door to the arctic entry, cold air wafted in and instantly condensed to ice fog. Some wag behind me hollered, "Have a nice day." I looked around, but all I could see was the fog, so I fanned the door a couple of times to share the misery. The "nice day" crack was partly because of the temperature, but also because Vickie had said, ". . . will be in a body bag," not ". . . is in a body bag". That likely meant that Tim and I would have to do the bagging, so how nice a day it was would depend on the vintage of the body and how many pieces it was in.

When the state troopers called, they asked for me and I chauffeured them if I was available, but not because I'm the best pilot. There's a level of competence beyond which degrees are meaningless.

The troopers asked for me because I was the one they had conned into getting my private detective license. If you want one, you can get one, too. Just send a few hundred bucks to The School of Private Investigation; call me if you want the address. You read a couple of good books, take twenty open-book tests, and get an impressive diploma. You give the diploma and a few twenty-dollar bills to the state licensing bureau, and voilà, you're a shamus, a gumshoe, a private dick.

I took a lot of ribbing from the other pilots while I read the books. They asked whether I was learning to pick locks and spy through keyholes. The reality is the opposite. Since the object of most private investigation is to gather evidence that is admissible in court, you have to observe every law against trespass or invasion of privacy. Even jaywalking while you're on a case might get you thrown out of court. In the real world, most of the fictional detectives we grew up with would have gone to jail themselves while their suspects walked free.

It wasn't my detecting expertise the troopers wanted; it was the title. For instance, when a hot gun is submitted into evidence, the chain of custody has to be established. The jurors have to know that the gun the DA is waving in their faces is the same gun that the defendant waved at the victim. It sounds better if the troopers can say, "It was signed into the custody of Detective Price," rather than, "I gave it to Alex, the pilot." Notice, I said it *sounds* better.

It *isn't* better, many situations are illegal if you insist on getting technical, but you do what you have to do.

Bagging and loading bodies was not what I imagined when I decided to fly for a living. I was quoted twenty-five dollars an hour, which was very good in those days, and I pictured myself flying eight hours every day and getting rich by my standards. The catch-22 is that you are only paid for actual flying time, or are on half pay when you're on standby. Loading and unloading, changing the oil, or even a cylinder on your airplane, don't count.

Bagging a body and loading it is a two-man job. If the body is sprawled out on the ice it may take two men and a chain saw, or you may have to skip the bag. You don't bend a frozen corpse, and loading one can be a wrestling match even for two men.

Thirty below zero and a half-hearted gray daylight were about average. The absence of wind made it a good day. In Bethel at ten o'clock the sun was above the southern horizon, but a cloud cover masked its exact location. I stomped through the three- and five-inch snowdrifts on the frozen tarmac toward the first Cessna 206 on the flight line, my neoprene soles making squeaks that seemed to be amplified by the cold. Everything was frozen hard and brittle, so it was like walking inside a drum. The tarmac had been plowed, but that was yesterday. Snow in Bethel never stays put.

OTHER BOOKS FROM MCROY & BLACKBURN

MYSTERIES ✳ THRILLERS ✳ TALES OF THE BUSH ✳ TALES OF THE SEA
ADVENTURE ✳ TALL TALES ✳ SATIRE ✳ CHILDREN'S
HUMOR ✳ FICTION FROM THE NORTH
BOOKS FOR YOUNG AND OLD

Alaskans Die Young, by Susan Hudson Johnson
Battling Against Success, by Neil Davis
The Birthday Party, by Ann Chandonnet
Bucket, by Eric Forrer
Caught in the Sluice: Tales from Alaska's Gold Camps, by Neil Davis
Cut Bait, by C.M. Winterhouse
The Great Alaska Zingwater Caper, by Neil Davis
Keep the Round Side Down, by Tim Jones
The Long Dark: An Alaska Winter's Tale, by Slim Randles
Raven's Prey, by Slim Randles
The Wake-Up Call of the Wild, by Nita Nettleton

and coming soon:
Accessories are Everything in the Wild, by Nita Nettleton
In Dutch, by C. M. Winterhouse
The Red Mitten, by Sarah Jane Birdsall

www.alaskafiction.com

WHAT REVIEWERS SAY ABOUT M&B BOOKS

"*Alaskans Die Young* … is perfect for a relaxing read in an easy chair with a mug of steaming coffee on the side." —Shana Loshbaugh, *Fairbanks Daily News-Miner*

"Readers will enjoy the mystery, a wonderful cast of characters, and the Alaskan trivia they will absorb along the way [in *Raven's Prey*]. Randles' descriptive skills do credit to his deep knowledge of Alaska, the people, and the way of life, as he takes you along on the hunt of a lifetime in the far north." —Gail Skinner, *On the Scene* magazine

In this often humorous, but mostly matter-of-fact autobiographical novel [*Battlling Against Success*], Neil Davis tells the compelling story of growing up on a homestead near Fairbanks in the 1940s. It's hard to tell who's real and who's imaginary in this tale, for Davis does an outstanding job of bringing all the characters to life." —Melissa DeVaughn, *Alaska* magazine

"[*Bucket*] is a tale parents won't mind reading again and again...Eric Forrer's writing is as rich as an old-time fairy tale.... Eloise Forrer's unique, whimsical illustrations were done with colored carbon paper and an iron. The effect is something like woodblock printing, textured and lovely. Refreshingly, the book has no moral or lesson, except that sometimes you should let a story just take you away." —Donna Freedman, *Alaska* magazine

"C. M. Winterhouse, the newest writer on the Alaska mystery scene, has created a meandering and irresistible sometime sleuth in her debut novel, *Cut Bait*....Unlike some Alaska mysteries in which the only local color is the landscape, *Cut Bait* is filled with characters and situations that seem convincingly Alaskan." —Sandra Boatwright, *Fairbanks Daily News-Miner*

"[In *The Birthday Party*], Chandonnet's use of rhyme and meter keeps the story moving along toward the punch line..." —Nancy Brown, *Peninsula Clarion*

"Slim Randles can set one heck of a scene [in *The Long Dark*]... He just sinks you in there, and hopes you'll be willing to swim. The receptive reader is very willing to follow his lead... A quiet undercurrent of humor keeps the reader contentedly turning pages, looking forward to the next clever plot development. He has a good hand with a yarn." —Ann Chandonnet, *Juneau Empire*

"[*The Great Alaska Zingwater Caper*] is a very clever and very Alaskan story... Davis' book is a triumph because of how perfectly the characters fit their roles... It's an intriguing novel from a man who's been inside and seen the soft underbelly of the Alaska government, and wants you to know about it. And most important of all, as is so essential for life in Alaska, it is a great ride!" —Rich Seifert, *The Ester Republic*